8:17

N. COOPER

8:17

ISBN - Paperback: 978-0-6488510-7-3

ISBN - ebook: 978-0-6488510-8-0

Cover typography and design by 100 Covers

A catalogue record for this work is available from the National Library of Australia

FOR DEACON

PROLOGUE

"Hey James."

"Yes, Samantha?"

"Don't be stealin' the rest of my pizza while I'm doing the rounds again tonight."

A slight smile crept across the burly man's lips as he looked up from the patient chart he was working on.

"How many times do I have to tell you it wasn't me?"

Samantha couldn't help a familiar grin of her own. They'd worked together for a long time. He'd definitely eaten the pizza.

"Right… So I suppose one of the patients woke up just because they smelled Gino's special, came out here without being seen, ate it; then hopped back into bed after reattaching the monitors, which never went off by the way, and fell back into their nice peaceful coma?"

8:17

"It's possible," James returned with a shrug.

She snorted.

"Don't eat the pizza."

She headed down the hall towards the ward, but not before seeing him place a mischievous hand across his heart.

Technically, it was a quarter past eight in the morning, according to the oversized analogue clock on the wall. Having been on the night shift for the better part of two weeks now, it felt more like eight at night.

The morning shift should arrive at any moment, and there was just time to do the final checks before handing off her charges for the day. She couldn't help a small sigh as she entered the ward proper. The rain was back, pounding on the unnecessarily large window at the far end of the room. The view of Sydney's iconic skyline was actually quite good from up here on the third floor, at least when it wasn't pouring with rain.

She checked Mr Cooth's vitals on the first monitor before picking up the chart hanging at the end of his bed. His injuries had long since healed from the car crash which had landed him here. At least, the ones they understood. Yet here he lay, thirty-three years old; though if he ever woke, he would insist it had only been thirty-one.

She signed the chart and moved on.

The next patient was a dark-skinned Jane Doe, brought in by an ambulance eight months ago after being found robbed and beaten half to death. The police had done their best to identify the woman, but the thieves had taken her purse and any I.D. therein. A news segment complete with photos had appealed to the public for help, but no one had come forward, nor had anyone placed a missing person's report matching her description.

Samantha hated that. She always took extra care to make sure Jane was comfortable as she worked her rounds.

The next bed was empty. The patient who normally lay there had caught a break. His brother had won big in the lottery a few weeks back and organised permanent private home care as soon as the money cleared. It wasn't as good as waking up, but at least he would be around the people who loved him from now on.

She took the chart from the last bed on this side of the room. It was closest to the window and held a young patient named Sarah. The girl was only six years old, and looked as peaceful as if she'd just gone to sleep, just as she always did. Sarah's mother came in everyday to talk to her and brush her hair. Over the months her daughter had been in the hospital's care, Samantha had talked to her many times. They got on well and she wished she could do more for the amiable woman than just take care of her comatose child's physical needs.

A stray lock of auburn hair had fallen across the girl's face. The air-conditioning would do that sometimes. Samantha reached down to slip it back into place and jumped a foot in the air as the girl sat bolt upright; silent, and utterly still.

Samantha's heart tried to pound its way out of her chest, but as the shock wore off, she couldn't help but bark an ecstatic laugh.

"Sarah! Can you hear me? Sarah!"

There was no response.

"James!" Samantha hollered as she checked the Girl's pulse. "James! Get in here. Sarah's awake!"

Footsteps pounded down the corridor and skidded to a halt in the doorway.

"Saman…" The word choked off halfway, and she turned to see what had halted him at the door.

The clipboard holding Sarah's chart fell from numb fingers as she stared in bewilderment at the six other patients in the room, every one sitting up on their own, eyes locked ahead and making not a sound.

"James…" she whispered, half awed, half terrified.

This couldn't be happening. These people were here because there was no cure for the injuries they'd sustained. Even if they had all somehow miraculously recovered, and miraculously seemed an apt word at this point, there was absolutely no chance they would all do so at the same instant.

At any moment, Samantha was certain she would wake up and find out she'd fallen asleep at the nurse's station. That had to be it. This was just a dream…

A small hand tugged weakly on her sleeve, sending a chill all the way down Samantha's spine.

"Where am I?" a long unused voice asked from beside her.

C H A P T E R I

"And that's how the ferret was rescued from the drain. Back over to you, Mike."

The anchor-man looked less than impressed, and Jacinta Robbins could well understand why as she poured some cereal into a bowl and followed it with milk.

"Taxpayer dollars at work," she muttered to herself as she kept half an eye on the T.V.

The news had been especially boring today as she readied herself for work. Hopefully, that meant it would be somewhat calmer in the office as well. Of course, if the news could be relied upon to find out what was really happening in the world, people like her would be out of a job.

She glanced at the ornamental grandfather clock in the hallway, which ironically had come into her possession upon the reading of her maternal grandmother's will. Jacinta hurried to don a tailored charcoal suit jacket as she chewed another mouthful of her rushed breakfast. Fortunately, the office was only minutes away, and she still had a few moments before she needed to be out the door.

What was that the T.V. had just said?

Jacinta picked up the remote and hit the volume button as the confused presenter looked at a crew member for confirmation of the note he'd just been handed.

"Is this a joke?" he asked someone off screen in a most unprofessional manner.

Jacinta stopped eating as a voice from off camera answered.

"It's confirmed. Read the cue."

For a moment he looked blankly at where the crew member must be standing, his mouth opening to say something, then closing again as he shook his head.

"I'm sorry… I… I have to go. My sister…"

Without another word, the anchor-man stood, pushed his chair back and left the studio at just short of a run.

Jacinta raised her eyebrows in surprise and found herself willing someone at the station to hurry up and read whatever was on that note.

The co-host looked pole-axed as the anchor-man departed, but cleared her throat as the camera focused in on her, and struggled to follow the producer's instructions.

She took up the note herself, skimming it before shaking her head in confusion.

"I'm sorry," she said, forcing herself to focus in on the camera. "I want to apologise to our audience at home, but we've just received some extraordinary information."

She shuffled the papers on the desk for a moment as if unsure what to do, then took hold of herself and continued.

"Word has just reached us that at approximately eight-seventeen this morning, every coma patient at Saint Patrick's hospital in the western suburbs... woke at exactly the same moment. Furthermore, reports are now coming in from other hospitals around the city, confirming that this does not appear to be an isolated incident."

"Are you sure this is real?" she asked the producer again.

A moment later, a balding man in his late forties entered the frame with a pile of papers in his hand. He walked around the desk, deep in thought as he took up the anchor-man's vacant seat before giving the presenter a nod to say he would take it from here.

He gathered his thoughts for a moment as Jacinta watched the broadcast. She sat slowly in one of her plush lounge room chairs, breakfast forgotten as she watched on in growing disbelief.

"Ladies and Gentlemen, it is so rare that as reporters we get to impart any truly good news to the public. Having said that, I have in my hand confirmed reports from our correspondents in five major cities around the country, all of which say the same thing. At eight-seventeen this morning, local time, every coma patient in sixteen hospitals across all states and territories, which is all we've had a chance to confirm so far, has woken up. What could cause such an event is a complete mystery at this time, but as reports continue flooding in, there can no longer be any doubt..."

A man wearing earmuffs darted to the desk and gave the producer yet another note before disappearing back off screen.

The balding man sat back for a moment and then laughed abruptly before looking at the camera with an awed expression.

"As soon as we began confirming these reports, I instructed our staff here at the network to contact our correspondents around the world. In my hand, I have eyewitness accounts from London, Tokyo, New Delhi, and New York. Whatever this… phenomenon is, all indications are that it appears to have occurred on a global scale. Our best information now indicates that not only have coma patients in those cities woken, but that none of our correspondents anywhere has yet found one of these ill-fated souls still unconscious."

The man sat back for a moment as he ran out of words. Dead air filled the telecast for a long moment until Jacinta's phone rang, startling her with its jarring tone.

She shook her head to clear it of the thoughts running a hundred miles an hour, and answered.

"Jacinta here," she said, still trying to keep an ear on the news.

"Jacinta, good. Are you watching the news?"

"Yeah, I am. Just how real is this, Jeff?"

"That's what we need to determine. I'm pulling in all personnel. I need you in here now to help coordinate."

"All right… All right," she confirmed as she cleared her head. "I can be there in… six minutes,"

"Good. I'll have a briefing packet ready by the time you arrive."

Jacinta hung up the phone, switched off the T.V.,

and passing the counter took a last bite of her cereal, but didn't take time to empty the bowl.

Passing the linen cupboard, she opened the door and unlocked the hidden safe within, withdrawing her badge, key card, and sidearm before closing both doors. She grabbed the car keys off a peg on the wall above the hallway table as she passed and headed out without further delay.

So much for my calm day.

CHAPTER 2

Jacinta pulled into the underground parking space of an innocuous office block after using her key card to gain entry. Bringing the car to a halt, she killed the engine of her midnight blue, sixty-seven mustang convertible. It was a far cry from the unmarked, black four-wheel drives preferred by the A.T.U. for their very anonymity. She stepped out of the car and applied her thumbprint to the scanner being held out for her by an armed agent. The indicator flashed green a moment later, and the man nodded. He took her keys and summoned a junior agent to park it in the secured structure below.

Jacinta nodded and left him to do his job; she had one of her own.

Once in the lift, she scanned her retina for confirmation and hit the button for floor three. As she waited, she couldn't help but wonder why her agency had been called in on this.

The doors opened a moment later and Jacinta

stepped out into the controlled chaos that was the Anti-Terrorist Unit's major control centre. A waiting aide gave her a file as she stepped off the lift and walked through the bustle of agents and analysts going about their assigned tasks. That was all normal, though today there was an edge in the air which spoke of something big under way.

She ascended the three steps to an area of the floor unofficially known as the command deck and took a seat at her desk.

The file before her was thin.

Too thin, she thought as she broke the seal, flicking the file open to read the first of the three pages enclosed within.

She sighed as she finished. There wasn't much here that the morning news hadn't already disclosed. A few confirmations that the phenomenon had been global, to the best of the A.T.U.'s considerable knowledge. There was also an eyewitness report from a nurse who had been attending a ward of coma patients at the exact time of the awakening.

She stood, scanning the floor to locate her boss, Jeff Illum, Director of the A.T.U.

Without wasting time, she walked towards the portly man who looked to be somewhere in his mid-fifties, and had since she'd met him nearly two decades before. He looked up as she approached, the ceiling lights reflecting off his perfectly bald head.

"Good, you're here. Have you had a chance to get up to speed yet, Jacinta?"

"Yes. But there's not much there. Is this all we have?"

"So far, but reports are still coming in from all over the globe. This one's a real mess."

"Sir, a question?" Jacinta asked formally.

Jeff looked at her for an instant, then nodded.

"Why have we been asked to look into this? I can't imagine a terrorist group either having the capabilities of making… whatever this is, happen. Or having any inclination to do so even if they could."

Jeff stood as he thought for a moment.

"Given the scale of this event, the Prime Minister has ordered all agencies to use their full resources to identify its origins. To be blunt, I don't think this has anything to do with terrorists any more than you do. It hasn't been ruled out yet though, so let's get that done so we can get on with the actual business this department is mandated for."

"Very well," Jacinta frowned in thought.

"All right. I guess we can start off monitoring the

chatter from known groups and see if any of them are talking about this morning. They may not be directly involved, but assuming this isn't some bizarre natural event, a project on this scale would require massive resources and personnel. Someone we know must have had dealings with an underground organisation big enough to pull this off without alerting every intelligence community on the planet."

Jeff nodded in approval.

"Good, get your people working on that angle, then I want you down at Saint Patrick's Hospital interviewing the patients and staff. Also, take a squad, and Bernard. Have him run every test he can think of on the patients, both physiological and psychological. Use the hospital's equipment if you need to, and make sure none of them leave. Until we have a better understanding of what's going on, procedure dictates that subjects under investigation could pose some level of threat."

Jacinta nodded in agreement and walked back to her desk. She pressed a button on her intra-office phone and waited for the surgery to answer.

"Greeman here," a distracted voice came through the line.

"Doctor, Jacinta Robins. We need you to conduct a full examination of the coma patients."

8:17

"How full?" the elderly man enquired.

"Have anything you think you'll need which can't be found at Saint Patrick's Hospital packed and sent for a complete psychological and physiological workup. Meet team alpha in the garage in five minutes."

"Acknowledged," he replied before cutting the link.

Pressing another button on the phone, Jacinta opened a line to her lead tactical team.

"Jameson. We're going to Saint Patrick's. Have your team meet Doctor Greeman and myself in the garage in five minutes. This should be a standard containment op, but I don't want any surprises."

"Five minutes. Yes ma'am."

Jacinta hit the button a bit too hard as she broke the link. It always irritated her when he called her ma'am. She suspected Jameson did it on purpose, though he would no doubt deny it if pressed.

Those tasks seen to; she left her desk again. Taking a folder and pen from the top drawer, she went to see her core group of analysts, whose work area was next to her own.

"Gather round people," she told them in a slightly raised voice. They did so without delay.

"Does anyone have new information as yet?"

No one spoke up, just as she'd expected. They were all far too well trained to keep fresh developments from their superiors.

"Alright, until further evidence presents itself, we are working under the assumption that this is not a natural occurrence. Therefore, I want you to analyse chatter from known groups or individuals about where someone might have obtained the resources or labour force necessary to carry out an event of today's magnitude. I consider it highly probable that someone with whom we are already familiar would have had dealings with such a far-reaching group. Find out whom."

She motioned the team to go back to work and headed over to the lift. She was nearly there when Jeff called out, silencing the office.

"Jacinta, one of the patients at Saint Patrick's just tried to escape, nearly killing a security guard in the process. Get down there now."

She began to run.

CHAPTER 3

Jacinta hurried to the front desk of Saint Patrick's Hospital. Jameson and Greeman flanked her as she marched through the lobby. The rest of Jameson's team brought up the rear.

The trained agents, with their full tactical gear and automatic weapons, created a formidable impression on the civilians in the lobby. Several people made a beeline for the exit.

"If you are not in need of emergency medical care, please exit the building in an orderly fashion. There is a developing situation in this building, but no immediate threat," Jameson announced in a loud but calm voice.

Every instinct Jacinta owned screamed at her that it was a lie.

On the drive here, Jeff had radioed her team to tell them that several other hospitals were also reporting sporadic acts of violence from the awakened patients.

Thankfully for her, those would be the problems of other teams, and the police at large.

Her orders had been changed in light of these violent acts, and were now to confine and interrogate the patients. The interview and test protocol had been discarded as the violent escape attempts continued.

A tall, dark-skinned woman intercepted Jacinta on her way across the lobby and held out a hand.

"Agent Robbins. I'm Aleda Roberts, Director of Saint Patrick's. Your office informed us you were on the way. Please come with me."

Jacinta shook the offered hand without coming to a full stop and allowed Aleda to show her to the lifts.

"The coma patients have all been secured," she continued without hesitation. "We had to sedate two of them, but the others seem cooperative enough. Even so, we've moved them all to the secure wing for the time being."

"Good, you did the right thing," Jacinta replied. "Now tell me about the attack. What motivated it?"

"I wasn't there myself, but I'm told that the patient in question asked to be allowed to go to the bathroom. When a nurse tried to get her back to the ward, she became uncooperative, then made a run for it. Security attempted to stop her, but she'd picked up a scalpel somewhere. Before they knew what they were dealing with, she'd cut one man's hamstring right through to the bone and stabbed another in the lung. The only reason she didn't get further was that a pair of off-duty cops had just come in to see a friend. They were able to subdue her long enough for Doctor Gera to administer a sedative and place her in restraints. When two other patients started expressing a strong desire to leave immediately afterwards, I ordered them all moved to the secure wing under guard. At least until we can figure out what's happening to them."

The lift door opened as they approached, and Aleda called out to an exiting orderly to hold it.

The four of them entered, followed by four of the armed agents, and after the doors closed, the lift began to move.

"Tell me," Jacinta said after a moment. "The wounds your people suffered in the attack, they seem very specific. What was the patient's state of mind during the assault? Was she frenzied? Enraged? Methodical?"

Aleda just raised an eyebrow.

"From what the two officers who restrained her told me, she was completely calm the entire time…

Even when she was fighting them. It sounds strange, but I very much doubt those wounds were intended to kill. She immobilised the first guard, and the wound to the second man was serious, but not life threatening given the quick response time of the doctors. He's still in surgery, but I'm told his prognosis is optimistic."

The lift door rolled open, and Aleda led them down a short corridor and through a pair of locked checkpoints. Beyond, an isolated nurse's station served the few secured rooms the hospital kept for treating dangerous or highly contagious patients.

In front of the nurse's station, a dozen small transparently fronted rooms lay in a row. Seven of them were occupied. In one, a woman lay strapped to a table, unconscious, and in the adjoining room, a balding man of middling age also slumbered. The others were awake. A young girl, no more than six or seven, sat perched on the edge of a bed in front of them, her body language frightened.

Jacinta hadn't expected that.

She shook her head to clear it. There was something going on here that no one understood yet. According to the intel Jeff had sent them enroute, the proportion of awakened patients across the city attempting escape and committing acts of violence was far higher than should be expected.

8:17

"Is there anything else I need to know before we get started?"

Aleda shook her head.

"In all honesty, it hasn't even been an hour since the patients all woke up. We've taken basic bloodwork, but we're still waiting for the results."
"All right. This is Doctor Greeman. He has full authority to run all practical tests he feels necessary on the patients to discover what has occurred this morning. I'll need your staff to assist him in his efforts and expedite the use of any hospital equipment he needs to accomplish this."

"Wait a minute, these are our patients..." Aleda interjected.

"Not anymore. The sheer scope of this morning's events makes this an issue of national security. Until we get some solid answers, Greeman will oversee their care."

"It's a pleasure to be working with you," the elderly Doctor spoke up as he put out a hand for Aleda to shake, trying to smooth things over.

Aleda eyed him sideways, but shook his hand despite her obvious misgivings.

A button on the intercom blinked, and Aleda pushed it a little too hard.

"What is it?"

"You wanted to know when the first of the families arrived," a thin voice spoke from the other end.

Jacinta shook her head before Aleda could speak.

"Not until I've questioned them."

Aleda stared at her for a second as if about to object, but then sighed.

"Have James meet them in the lobby and escort them to the coma ward for now. I'll get to them as soon as I can. Oh, and have someone escort Samantha up to the secured wing."

"You got it," the voice responded before the speaker clicked off.

"Samantha was standing over that girl's bed when she woke," Aleda commented as she pointed to the child perched on the bed in the room across from the desk.

"Gave the poor woman the fright of her life when she turned around and saw them all sitting up like that, I'm told."

"No doubt," Jacinta agreed, privately glad that it hadn't been her.

"You need to let us go," a small voice spoke up from inside the sealed room across the hall.

8:17

Jacinta shared a glance with Aleda, and the two women approached the transparent wall. A chart hanging from a hook proclaimed the girl's name as Sarah Winthrop.

"We have done nothing wrong. Why are we in here?"

"Sarah, is it?" Jacinta asked the small, auburn-haired girl as she knelt, bringing the two of them eye to eye.

The girl hesitated, then nodded.

"Well, Sarah, we were a bit taken by surprise the way you all woke up together. These nice doctors just have to make sure you're all okay before we let you go home."

The child studied her for a moment through the glass, her expression as unreadable as the best of poker players.

"You're lying."

"Why do you think that?" Jacinta returned.

"I can tell. There will be consequences if you do not release us. This will be your only warning," the little girl announced.

Jacinta glanced at Aleda, but got only a puzzled look from the hospital administrator.

"Why would you say that, Sarah?"

"Say what? Is my mother here yet? I want to go home now," she added.

Jacinta just looked at the child for a moment, receiving a disturbingly unchildlike stare in response.

She stood, joined by Aleda, and walked the few steps back to Greeman, where she spoke in a hushed tone.

"Do whatever tests you need to, doctor. Something is very wrong here. We can't risk letting these people back into the general population until we know what it is."

"She's just a child," Aleda objected. "And one who has just woken up from an eight-month coma at that. Is it any wonder she's upset at being locked up?"

Jacinta just looked at the other woman for a moment.

"Did she seem aggravated to you just now?"

Aleda shook her head slowly in the negative. "No, I suppose she didn't"

"Confused?" Jacinta asked. "Tired? Out of sorts? Was she throwing a tantrum?"

Again, Aleda was forced to shake her head.

"Exactly. What she did just do was make a demand

backed up by a threat in a calm, capable manner. That little display should be far beyond the emotional maturity I would expect from, as you say, a six-year-old who has just woken from an extended coma. Especially one who has found herself forcibly locked up without seeing anyone she knows. Nothing about that interaction sits right with me. Get started, doctors. We need to know what we're dealing with here."

Greeman motioned for Aleda to show the way, but as he moved to follow her, Jacinta grabbed his arm before he could leave.

"Work quickly. It won't be long before their families start screaming for their release. As of right now, we have no legitimate way to hold them save falling back on the public safety and national security lines. The media won't let that stand long where children are involved. Let me know the moment you have something."

Greeman nodded and moved off to follow Director Roberts.

Jacinta turned and regarded the drugged patient who had assaulted the hospital staff in her bid for escape, then motioned toward an orderly at the nurse's station.

"Wake her up. We need to have a chat."

CHAPTER 4

"I know all that, Jeff. I just can't help thinking this is a mistake of monumental proportions. We still have no answers as to why these people woke up, or why several of them were hell bent on escape, even to the point of committing violence during that first hour. And no one even wants to talk about why several of the families overseas seem to think that the awakened are very different now than before they ended up in their comas."

Jeff looked at her for a moment before shaking his head.

"I believe you Jacinta, but if you want me to act, you have got to give me something more concrete than your bad feelings. Otherwise, my hands are tied."

She sighed. "That's just it, Jeff. Something happens that has never been recorded once in almost six thousand years of worldwide written history, and we're so enamoured of the result that no one is taking sufficient time to get to the root of the cause."

"In principle, I agree. You know I do. And I'd love to spend the next year getting to the bottom of all this, but I have my orders. Unless you can give me something by the end of the day that at least points to terrorist connections, this agency's involvement in the awakening is at an end."

Jacinta ground her teeth as he spoke.

"Then I'd better get to Saint Patrick's.

"Come on Jacinta, what do you hope to gain by interrogating them for what, the eighth time?"

"If I knew that, I wouldn't need to interrogate them at all. Look, you said I have till the end of the day."

"Jacinta…"

"Jeff. Don't ask me to do less than I can."

She waited for a moment, then received a terse nod.

"They get released at five. No delays unless there is a major breakthrough you clear with me first, understood?"

"Understood."

*   *   *

It was ten to five, and her time was up. In a few minutes, orderlies would come in and take a final set of vitals before the government released these people into the community. Why she wasn't happy about the situation was a question Jacinta had been asking herself all day. She knew she should be, but even after all this time, something just didn't sit right. She had spent most of the day with Sarah, trying to get any spark of the forcefulness the little girl had shown that first day to reappear. It had been a waste of time.

She had one last card to play. Jacinta knew she could be reprimanded if it backfired, but it was all she had as she stood in front of the thick glass wall of the isolation rooms in Saint Patrick's Hospital once again.

"Tell me why you attacked those guards, Victoria."

The mugging victim had been a Jane Doe before the awakening, but was now known to be one Victoria Jones. She had been on a backpacking holiday from the UK when ill luck had changed her life forever. It was she who had attacked the guards in a very nearly successful attempt to escape the hospital after waking. She did her best to hide it, but it was clear to Jacinta that of all the awakened patients, Victoria was still the most eager to be free.

"Oh, for the love of… How many times do I have to tell you I don't even remember doing those things?

How do I even know you're not just making them up, 'ey?" the tall dark-skinned woman replied in heavily accented English.

"I can show you the security footage if you like, or you can just wait and see it at your trial."

"My trial?!" Victoria shouted in alarm. "What kind of messed up country is this? I come down under to this supposedly friendly country for a holiday. I get robbed, beaten, end up in a coma, and now you want to put me on trial? I don't think so!"

"I'm sorry, but the evidence is clear. We have the attack on video and multiple eyewitnesses to confirm the event. The others will leave here shortly, but you can look forward to spending a long time behind bars for assault with a deadly weapon, amongst other charges. Of course, the doctors say that you were all disoriented when you woke, but I just don't believe it. You see, the wounds you inflicted on the guards were precise, methodical, not at all the work of a disoriented individual. I intend to see you put away for a long time for that assault."

For a long moment, Victoria just stared daggers at Jacinta through the thick glass.

"What do you want for my freedom?" She eventually asked, her voice low and flat, all trace of an accent gone.

It made Jacinta's blood run cold as she noticed all the other patients watching the exchange with gazes as flat as the one Victoria was now giving her.

"Victoria…"

It was only a single word, and spoken by the smallest of the awakened, Sarah, but the effect was instantaneous. Victoria stepped back and lowered her eyes.

"Whatever you think is best, Agent Robbins," she meekly replied, accent once again firmly in place.

Without a word, the others all abruptly stepped away from the glass and resumed their various activities. It reminded Jacinta of nothing so much as a group of children who knew they were behaving badly and had just heard a parent about to enter the room.

A second later, the lift down the corridor dinged its arrival. Jacinta looked at it in consternation as four orderlies and Director Illum exited, oblivious to the patients' prescient actions.

She looked back at Victoria, who had the slightest of knowing smiles on her lips.

Without another word, Jacinta walked over to Jeff and pulled him aside.

"We have to talk. Now."

CHAPTER 5

It had been three months today since they had released the awakened, and the news wouldn't let her forget it.

Jacinta shook her head slightly in anger as she remembered the heated argument she'd had with Jeff in Saint Patrick's isolation ward.

'There's something very wrong with these people.' That's what she'd told him, relating the conversation she'd just had with Victoria, and the others' strange behaviour just before he'd exited the lift.

He hadn't gone so far as to call her a liar. Nor had he accused her of making up a story in order to keep the awakened in the isolation cells a few more days. But he hadn't done anything about it either.

"Just look at the video feed!"

Jeff had sighed and even agreed, but maddeningly, the video system had gone offline halfway through her conversation with Victoria and had captured nothing unusual. The feed had returned a few minutes later.

It was an old building, bad wiring or something. At least that's what she kept telling herself when she saw Victoria's knowing grin in her mind's eye in the days since their release.

With no hard evidence as to why they had to be kept locked away as they were, Jeff had seen no option but to release them as planned.

It wasn't until she helped escort them downstairs that she fully understood his reticence to give her any more time. The hospital lobby was crowded from one end to the other. Reporters jockeyed for position, clamouring to get the first snaps of the awakened being reunited with loved ones. Rows of smiling or weeping family members had come to collect their long absent relatives.

Security was out in force, and a cordon separated those with a right to be there from the media circus surrounding their moment of joy. Around all the chaos, the hospital was still trying to function, and several out-patients were looking quite irritated at the noise and bustle. When one of the cameramen tripped over a man sporting a broken leg, security forcibly ejected him. The commotion caused several photographers to snap pictures his way before returning to their original quarry.

After they had reunited the awakened with their relatives, there was a short but uninspired speech from the mayor. Then she'd been forced to watch as the seven of them and their families simply walked out the door, powerless to stop what she'd known in her gut was a terrible mistake.

"Jacinta," Jeff said as he approached her desk, breaking her out of her reverie.

Her eyes snapped up. She hadn't hidden her irritation well enough apparently as she saw the director purse his lips and frown, though he made no more comment than that.

He didn't need to, and she sighed, partly in irritation at herself and partly at the situation. After all, he really hadn't had any other option.

"Sorry. You know how much I hate questions without answers, and this…"

He nodded, letting it drop. They'd worked together for a long time.

"On that note, here's something unrelated to occupy your mind. I want you to look over this report and see what you make of it."

She took the folder he proffered and flicked open

the first page. Jeff waited as she read the summary, and Jacinta felt a slight frown alight on her brow as she came to the end.

"I don't understand. This tip came from Harberg Fabrications itself?

"Yes, they manufacture large industrial orders all the time. The plant manager thought to alert us when a new customer began to order specific, custom parts even the company didn't understand the function of."

"Couldn't they just ask?" Jacinta responded.

"They did, but that resulted in the customer walking out of their offices, the latest order she'd been about to make still unplaced. The manager, one Leyland Edelson, isn't expecting her to return."

"So you want me to find out what they're building?"

"Yes, but discretely. Right now, all we know is that we don't know anything. There may be nothing more here than a colossal modern art project. However, the obvious secrecy this buyer seems to be working under suggests otherwise. Either way, we need to determine if this is in any way a threat."

"All right," Jacinta agreed. "I'll start my team working up potential uses for the ordered parts and follow up with the plant manager about the buyer."

* * *

"So is there anything else you can tell me about this woman?" Jacinta asked Mr. Edelson, the plant manager at Harberg Fabrications.

"I'm afraid not. As I mentioned on the phone, our security system was down that day for several hours. There's simply no footage to show you."

"What about her previous visits? Do you have footage from those?"

"I'm afraid we only keep the lobby footage for a week, and aside from this morning, she hasn't been here for longer than that. The corporate suite is a secure room and has no surveillance devices for confidentiality reasons."

Jacinta sighed. It was hard for her to fathom that in this day and age, a company such as this would not have tighter security measures in place.

"Very well then, I was hoping some footage might have turned up, but due to our phone conversation, I've brought one of our sketch artists here with me today. Would you mind working with him to give us an idea of what this woman looked like?"

"Of course," Edelson replied. "Anything I can do to help."

"All right," Jacinta said as she stood, "If you remember anything else, or if you work out what these parts are for, please don't hesitate to call."

She passed him a card with her office's contacts.

Edelson stood and shook her hand as she left. As she passed Agent Clarc in the corridor, she gave a nod to the sketch artist, telling him to go in.

* * *

Her driver pulled into the official underground entrance of the A.T.U. complex. It was a block and a half away from the non-descript office complex entrance she entered every morning. Also a secure building, that complex existed as a cover so agents like her could approach A.T.U. headquarters via a concealed tunnel to park their private vehicles. Jacinta made the short trip through security and over to a conference room where she summoned her team. She'd learned little of use at Harberg Fabrications.

"What do we have?" She asked the four analysts in her group.

There were looks all around, but no one spoke.

"I see..." Jacinta frowned, a certain unease chewing at the back of her mind. The four people in front of her had an average I.Q. of nearly one hundred and sixty. If they were stumped, this was either nothing at all, or something very bad indeed.

"All right, let's go over it from the beginning," Jacinta said as she motioned for them to take their seats.

"An unknown woman orders several custom fabricated parts made of high-grade steel over the course of several months. She appears to be a private citizen, and only representing herself, not a company. She either wants or needs more parts as she was about to place another order when the plant manager questions her on their use. This causes her to leave Harberg Fabrications without further conversation. At this point, the manager becomes suspicious and calls us. What do we make of this?"

There was a ding, and Andrea, a middle-aged woman with a matronly appearance and fiery red hair opened her laptop while the others considered the situation.

"Diane Jarmain is a false name," Andrea announced without preamble. "Our mystery buyer has no driver's licence, passport, or social security number."

"But enough fake documentation and money for Harberg Fabrications to go ahead with her orders," Mike Cowl added in his usual offhand manner, as though his mind were somewhere else entirely.

"We have no video of the buyer, and there is no delivery address as she picked up the parts from Harberg herself. No one bothered taking the plates of the trucks she used since the buyer was there in person. The company had a number for her, but it turned out to be a prepaid mobile, and has since been disconnected. This woman has taken great pains to keep her identity hidden. I don't like where this is heading," Jacinta told them brusquely.

"We need to find out what other potential pieces go with this equipment," Seth Gabel mused aloud. "Right now, we have some jigsaw pieces and no box lid to guide us. Without knowing what the overall picture should look like, we may never know what these parts are for."

"Good, chase that up Seth. Contact every company that deals in custom industrial parts in the city and see if she's placed orders anywhere else. Also, as soon as Agent Clarc gets back to us with her image, circulate it and see if she's placed any orders under different names."

Seth nodded and left the room.

8:17

"What about you Lindel, anything to add?" Jacinta asked her youngest analyst.

At twenty-six, Lindel Harding already had degrees in mechatronics, structural engineering, and applied physics. Her bio claimed she was one of the ten smartest people in the country, and only consulted at the A.T.U. on cases where advanced machinery was in play. As luck would have it, she had been in the city already, and a chopper was sent out to retrieve her as soon as this investigation had become a priority.

"Not at this point. With only these pieces to go on, anything I could say would only be wild speculation."

Jacinta looked her in the eye. "Give us your best guess then."

Lindel shifted in her seat, uncomfortable with being put on the spot.

"If there were several other pieces, perhaps a housing of some kind… The few schematics we have seem to suggest a device with an aperture at one end. It could be the framework for an articulated stand, say for a medium sized antenna dish or large telescope. Or it could be something more sinister, such as an enormous gun or cannon. With the small amount of information we have, there's no way to know."

"All right, we'll see if Seth turns anything up on that front. In the meantime I want the rest of you working on the identity of our mystery buyer."

Jacinta stood, and the others followed her back out into the main work area to their respective desks. It was only a minute later when Director Illum walked over, not hurrying, but clearly heading for her. He looked like he meant business as he came to a halt in front of her desk.

"I'm afraid I owe you an apology Jacinta. Agent Clarc just sent through this sketch of our buyer from Harberg Fabrications. I think you'll recognise her."

Jacinta took the piece of paper he offered. She looked at it, then placed it very carefully on the desk, struggling not to make some acid remark as she leant back in her chair.

"Victoria," was all she managed in the end.

CHAPTER 6

"Listen up, people!" Director Illum called out, bringing the entire A.T.U. office to a standstill. "I have just received confirmation that a large amount of reactor grade nuclear material has been stolen from our power plant here in the city. As of this moment, locating and recovering this material is our only priority. Clear your boards of all current assignments and let's find these thieves before they can do whatever it is they're planning. Briefing packets are going out to team leaders' stations as we speak. Get to work."

Jacinta waved her team over as she opened the document Jeff had just sent out. What little information it offered wasn't good. Forty-eight fuel rods had disappeared from their secure holding facility at the plant. The guards had seen nothing, had not even known a robbery was occurring at the time. To make matters worse, the entry was visible from several workstations. All their accounts confirmed the guards had not left their posts or allowed anyone to enter during the shift. According to Jeff's document, the vault where they kept the rods only had one direct entrance. There were no signs of forced entry inside the room, neither had tunnels been dug, nor explosives used. The only oddity was that for eleven minutes between one and two p.m. the security system across the entire plant had been down.

Jacinta looked up to see her team had arrived.

"All right. Andrea, I want damage projections and casualty estimates for devices which can be assembled from combinations of up to forty-eight nuclear fuel rods customised for a type three industrial reactor."

The analyst nodded and left.

"Seth, I want a list of every possible use for these materials, criminal or otherwise."

"Coming right up," He replied before heading back to his desk.

"Mike, comb our sources, see if there is any chatter about a big attack or an upcoming sale."

"I'll have it in an hour," he said as he left.

"Lindel, you're coming with me to the power plant. The way the security system went down is a little too reminiscent of what happened at Harberg Fabrications for my liking. I want you to see if you can retrieve any data at all. If not, at least try to find out how and why the system failed, then came back up after the thieves were gone."

Lindel nodded thoughtfully but didn't move.

"Was there something else?"

"I was just thinking, even if there is no footage of the thieves at the plant, they had to get the rods out somehow. If we move quickly enough, we might be able to follow the radiation trail with a sensitive enough Geiger counter. I think I can get hold of a prototype design that one of my colleagues has been working on."

Jacinta smiled. "Lindel you never cease to amaze. Have someone meet us with the equipment at the plant. Gather up whatever else you need and meet us in the garage in two minutes."

Lindel left to do just that, and Jacinta hit the appropriate button on her secure phone.

"Jameson, we may have a lead on the missing materials. Meet me with a fully geared tactical team and armoured transportation in the garage immediately."

"Yes ma..." was all he got out before Jacinta cut the line.

Hitting another button, she filled Jeff in on Lindel's possible thread and he authorised the assets and investigation.

Jacinta looked around. Seeing all was in order, she typed a two-line memo to her team informing them of her absence, before heading to the garage with Lindel in tow.

* * *

Across town and sixteen minutes later, Jacinta, Lindel, and Jameson were entering the giant nuclear facility which powered half the city. The team of elite soldiers Jameson commanded were right on their heels, their body armour and fully automatic weapons making a formidable impression.

As they approached the front entrance, an officious little man with a bad comb-over and overly expensive suit for a day at work greeted them.

"I'm Alan Dias, plant administrator. Right this way please," he said in a no-nonsense tone which fit not at all with his appearance.

"We've set up an area for you in the control room where you will have access to all the relevant materials. Is there anything you require, agent?"

8:17

"Robbins," Jacinta replied. "These are Agent's Harding, and Jameson. We have some equipment on the way. Please see it reaches us immediately upon arrival," Jacinta replied.

"Of course," Dias answered as he led them up a flight of stairs and into the well-equipped room full of monitors and stations which oversaw the operation of the plant.

"Get started," Jacinta told Lindel as Dias motioned them to an empty station which connected to the security systems.

"Is there anything at all you can tell me about the theft that wasn't in the report?" Jacinta probed, hoping the manager could offer some extra insight which hadn't been included in Jeff's short briefing document.

"I wish there were, but short of my entire staff being corrupt, I don't understand how this could have happened. There is only one exit to that storage vault, and every witness has offered the same story; it was never breached. Yet the rods were accounted for visually at the start of the shift and at each hour afterward, but gone after the security feed came back up."

"Why wasn't the stockpile being manually observed while the security system was down?"

Dias just looked at her for a long moment before speaking. "Perhaps in hindsight that would have been prudent, but you must understand that the bunker is a fortress. Its entrance is visible from no less than eight different security checkpoints, not to mention a myriad of other manned stations. We also employ several seismometers across the site which alert us to even the slightest subsurface tremor. Were someone to try drilling into the bunker from underground our equipment would warn us before the thieves got within a hundred metres of the containment room. In addition, the blackout of the security feeds was not local to the bunker. We simply had no reason at the time to suspect anything was amiss beyond a simple I.T. malfunction."

"These seismometers, could they have been affected by whatever brought down the other feeds?" Jacinta probed.

"Not possible Agent Robbins. The information they send to the central computers could perhaps be compromised, but the sensors in the machinery itself are analogue, and print out to hard copy as soon as vibration is detected. I already had all the base units checked. The readings on all units were continuous over the period of the outage and never altered from baseline."

"Very well, and you're certain that these were the

only materials taken?" Jacinta asked after a moment.

"Yes. The moment we detected the theft I ordered a visual check of all remaining materials and notified the appropriate authorities."

Jacinta pursed her lips in frustration. "All right, take me to the bunker. Lindel, keep working here and let me know the moment you have something. Jameson, leave one man with Lindel, the rest with me."

Lindel nodded and went back to examining a segment of code on the computer screen as Jameson motioned to one of his men to stay behind.

"This way, please," Dias prompted, and Jacinta followed him back out the same way they'd come in.

As they left the main building, an armed escort vehicle preceded a van with the markings of a local university and pulled up in front of them. Jacinta walked towards it while the driver exited, and seeing their approach, the young man called out.

"I'm looking for Lindel Harding?"

"Jacinta Robbins, Lindel works for me," she told him as she shook his hand.

"You have the equipment she asked for?"

"In the back," the skinny young man answered.

"And you can operate it I take it?"

"Of course, I designed it. Name's Simon by the way."

"Good. Bring whatever you need with you, Simon."

She waited for him to go around the back and remove an apple tray sized box with what appeared to be a microphone attached to a cord at one end.

As soon as he was ready the three of them set off, accompanied by Jameson and his team.

When they arrived at a ramp delving into the poured concrete ground across the compound, four men with automatic rifles greeted them, each standing stiffly at attention.

"Is this the usual guard complement?" Jacinta asked Dias as they approached.

"As of today it is," he replied grimly. "Until now only two men were present on any given shift. Though as I said, this entrance is visible from many points across the compound."

Jacinta turned around. Scanning the area, she was forced to agree, no one was getting in here in broad daylight without being seen by at least half a dozen witnesses.

"Has anyone been inside since the discovery was made?" Dias ask one of the guards.

"No one in or out since the confirmation team finished sir, as per your orders," the serious brown-haired guard replied.

"Very well," Dias answered before continuing past the armed men and inputting his personal code in the door at the bottom of the ramp. With a loud click, the vault-like structure unlocked and slowly began to retract.

* * *

It was a quick trip as the group walked the length of a short corridor, through another set of secured doors, and into the main storage room. In it were two sets of heavy tables containing six thick metal crates each. The rows of tables led away from them towards the back of the room, though the last slot in the right column was conspicuously empty. Dias motioned them forward and soon they arrived at the unremarkable space where forty-eight nuclear fuel rods should have been housed in their lead-lined crate.

"What's that?" Jacinta asked as she pointed to a hole in the left wall just large enough for one of the crates to fit.

"Conveyor," Dias responded after a glance at

where she had motioned. "We haven't moved any materials around the surface of the compound since shortly after nine-eleven. This one only goes one place, the main reactor room. On the other wall the conveyor moves from the secure loading dock to here, in this direction only."

"I take it the chutes have been cleared?" Jacinta asked, already sure of the answer.

"Of course. It was the first thing we checked. There are guards stationed at the other end of either chute rather than in here due to radiation concerns. They also reported seeing nothing out of the ordinary, as did the dock and reactor workers. In fact there was no movement scheduled today on either belt, and the security sensors in both cases remain untripped."

"I thought the security system was down during the theft?"

"Indeed. However, the belts use physical sensors due to the higher-than-normal radiation levels. They would have worked even without the computer system operating, and in case you weren't aware, we only lost the feeds, not the power itself."

Jacinta gave a small sigh as she tried to make sense of Dias' report.

"All right Simon, fire up your gizmo and see what you can tell us," she said at length.

8:17

The technician gave a nervous cough and a dubious smile as he turned on the machine.

"Is there a problem?" Jacinta enquired.

"I don't know," Simon answered. "I wasn't expecting this many crates… It could throw off the readings."

"Is there anything we can do to help?"

Simon thought for a moment before turning to Dias.

"It might be useful to know what the normal procedure is for storing the crates so I can rule out some of the readings I'm about to take."

"Of course," Dias responded. "The procedure is simple. When we receive a crate, a pair of technicians will enter the way we came in. They will take the trolley in the corner nearest the door and place it at the end of the incoming chute. The crate will slide off the conveyor onto the trolley, which is then moved to the empty slot reserved for it, and we deposit the crate in the appropriate slot."

"What about when the crates go to the reactor room?" Simon enquired.

"The exact opposite, on the other side of the room."

"So there shouldn't be any movement towards the door side of the room then?"

"Not past the first crate slots, no," Dias confirmed.

"Good, I'll start there then," Simon told them before heading back the short distance towards the first of the crates.

Dias waited tensely while the technician took some baseline readings, then started scanning the room in the door's direction.

"Can we open these gates up, I need to confirm that the chutes are empty for my report," Jacinta asked Dias politely. In truth she wanted the confirmation for herself more than any paperwork she would have to file later, and there was sure to be a lot of it.

Dias nodded and walked the short distance to the chute before inputting a code in the control panel. The gate moved toward the floor and Dias activated his radio.

"Director Dias to dock supervisor."

There was a brief wait.

"Kendell here sir, what do you need."

"Please open the dock chute gate so Agent Robbins can confirm the chute is clear."

"Doing it now, sir," came the crisp response.

A moment later the square chute was bathed in

light as the dock gate lowered, giving a clear and unobstructed view through to the other side.

Jacinta took a compact torch from her pocket and shone it down the short tunnel. Aside from the lump where the sensor Dias had mentioned was visible, the walls were intact and featureless. She switched off the torch and nodded, prompting Dias to radio for the gate to be closed before using the control pad to achieve the same at his end.

"Well, the good news is that I'm not picking up any trails leading to the entrance," Simon announced. "Looks like whoever took them didn't use the front door."

Dias looked at the ground for a moment in silence as a deep frown steadily took root on his face.

Jacinta understood. If the door hadn't been the exit point for the rods, it meant at least a couple, and probably more, of Dias' own people must have been involved in getting the materials out.

"Shall we," Jacinta motioned at the reactor chute as Simon continued his sweep.

It was enough, and Dias broke out of whatever dark thoughts he'd been harbouring as he strode across and opened the gate, radioing for the same on the other side.

Again light bathed the conveyor to reveal only an empty tunnel and a technician dressed in a protective suit on the other side.

Jacinta nodded to Dias and again the gates were closed.

By now Simon was finishing on the dock side of the room, steadily making his way back as he scanned the vacant slot where the crate full of nuclear materials should have been.

"I'm still getting a faint reading here," he reported. "Enough to be sure fissionable materials were present in the last twelve hours."

As he finished scanning the slot Simon walked around the back of the crate lines and stopped.

"Wait a minute," he said, halting them all in their tracks. "Why am I picking up a reading back here? Is there any reason for a crate to be moved beyond these slots?" He asked Dias, who frowned as he shook his head.

"Our policy is minimum movement of all materials, they go from chute to slot, across to the next slot when it becomes available, then directly to the reactor chute. There is no reason materials should be moved beyond the last row at any time."

"Well some have been," Simon commented as he

continued scanning, moving further and further towards the back of the room.

He walked slowly, waving the microphone-like device from side to side to make sure he stayed on track.

Eventually he came to the far wall and stopped, moving the scanner around with a perplexed expression.

"I don't understand," he muttered.

"What is it?" Jacinta demanded, breaking him out of his confused thoughts.

"I don't know," Simon answered. "According to these readings, materials were transported from the empty slot to this wall, but then the trail stops cold."

"Scan the wall." Jacinta ordered him without preamble.

"Dias, what's behind here?"

Dias looked thunderstruck for a moment, but recovered quickly. "Nothing, a six-inch lead wall behind which is solid rock. We're twenty feet underground here. There shouldn't be anything behind this wall."

"We need to bring in a ground penetrating radar to scan behind here for a tunnel. Just to be sure." She added as she saw Dias' protesting motion towards the unbroken or damaged six-inch lead plating.

"All right," he agreed, holding up his hands in surrender. "Best to be thorough."

As Dias reached for his radio, a voice came to life from next to her.

"Jameson, put Agent Robbins on!"

Jacinta almost snatched the radio off him at the panic in Lindel's voice.

"What's happening Lindel?" She demanded as soon as she could press the talk button.

"Jacinta, I need you in the control room. Right now!"

"Get us out of here," she told Dias as she took him by the arm and thrust him towards the access panel.

* * *

She crossed the compound at a dead run, bounding up the few short steps to the main entry. Jameson stayed with her step for step, along with three members of his team.

A guard at the front door moved to challenge them for a moment. Dias waved him off from behind them. The man was badly out of breath, but doing his level best to keep up with the trained agents.

8:17

Jacinta was forced to slow for a moment while the automatic doors opened, then sprinted up a flight of crowded stairs and across to the main control room. Jameson intentionally blocked her for a second as they reached the door, raising his machine gun and preceding her into the room.

Jacinta found it mildly irritating. However, being first through the door was part of his job description, so she drew her pistol and followed right on his heels, ready to provide whatever backup was needed. Lindel was not one to panic easily, and as Jacinta rounded the door with the three other agents in tow, she could only imagine what could have set the brilliant young woman so on edge.

Jameson was stalking the room, his men fanning out behind him as they scanned for any possible threat. Jacinta located Lindel, who was standing behind the same desk she'd been working at when they'd parted. The woman was white as a sheet, and she motioned Jacinta over to her.

"Are you all right?" Jacinta asked as she crossed the room, "What's happening?"

Apart from Lindel, there was no one else left in the control room except two confused technicians down by a desk at the far end of the room. Them and the man Jameson had left as her escort.

"I ordered them all out," Lindel said without preamble or excuse as Dias caught up, looked around with a frown, and joined them.

"You need to see this, Jacinta," she repeated as she motioned to the seat she'd been using.

"But there's no other threat?" Jacinta asked, a little disturbed now as to what Lindel had uncovered.

"Other threat? Oh, no, this is quite enough I should think."

Jacinta holstered her weapon as she called for Jameson and his men to stand down, then sat while Lindel played back the security footage she'd been working on.

The playback was a little fuzzy, but the vision was identifiable as being from the camera in the underground storage bunker they'd just been in.

"I won't go into technical detail right now, but I was able to use one of my programs to filter out enough interference from this security footage to make it… watchable. At first glance everything is as it should be, you can see the missing crate is still in place."

"What the..?" Jacinta exclaimed, almost jumping out of her seat as a man pushing a flatbed trolley simply strolled through the back wall of the building.

She was sure that once confirmed, it would prove to be the exact spot Simon had noted the strange readings. The man appeared to be humming as he tapped something on his wrist before efficiently loading the crate of nuclear fuel rods onto the trolley. Without hurrying, he spun the trolley around and touched the device on his wrist again. The man then strode back into the wall as though he were nothing more than a ghost. Aside from the very real crate of nuclear materials he had just wandered off with.

Lindel reached out and halted the playback.

Jacinta looked up at her for a long moment, trying to determine whether the usually sombre woman was having her on, while Dias just stood there in shock.

"But that's..." Jacinta finally got out.

"Yes. Quite," Lindel replied. "At least to our current understanding of physics."

Jacinta just sat there for a moment, at a loss how to proceed.

"All right, first things first. Dias, I'm officially classifying this video, which means this goes nowhere. You don't discuss it with your wife, your mother, or even myself unless someone with clearance initiates the conversation. Are we completely, totally, clear on this point?"

Dias looked at her for a moment before nodding.

"As if anyone would believe it anyway," he replied.

That in itself worried Jacinta greatly. Dias was not just a manager for the plant, but a trained and experienced physicist in his own right. Yet even he was struggling to believe what he'd just seen, or perhaps even that he had seen it at all.

"Good," Jacinta replied as she stood. "Lindel, make a hard copy and a backup of the file, then wipe any mention of this record from the system.

"Okay," She replied as she took back the seat.

"Dias. I want the back wall of that bunker taken apart, and the lead plates sent to the A.T.U. for study. Then I want the same for the rock behind it, if there is still any there."

"Of course Agent Robbins, you will have our full cooperation. I do have to clear all major works on this site with the minister first though."

"Not this time," Jacinta shook her head, "The A.T.U. has penultimate authority over all civilian government departments during times of national crisis. As of this moment we have confirmation that nuclear materials are missing, and in the hands of unidentified persons for reasons unknown, which certainly qualifies. Get the work started and I'll clear the paperwork with the minister from our end."

"You got it," Dias responded, his state of shock starting to wear off as he moved away, talking into his radio.

"Jameson, you and your men are to remain onsite until they get that wall off. Make sure there's nothing behind it except rock, then report in."

The tall man in full tactical gear nodded as Lindel stood.

"Ready," she announced.

"Good, we need to get back to A.T.U. headquarters, fill Jeff in on this mess, and formulate some kind of response. We'll send another car for your team," she added to Jameson as she turned and left the room, her team members following her lead just as she knew they would.

CHAPTER 7

"We've got satellites scanning the city for any suspicious activity. But with the lead time the thieves had, coupled with the fact that we have no idea as to their method of transport, we have little to no hope of finding them that way. I've got local enforcement scanning every speed, red light, ATM, and private security camera within a ten-block radius for the thief's face, but so far we've got nothing. Also, as criminal records came up with no matches, a facial recognition match is being run against the entire country right now in an attempt to identify our target. With no other parameters though, unless we get a lucky hit it will take precious time we don't have. To that end, a nationwide bulletin is going out within the next few minutes on all television and radio stations warning the public that we are on a heightened domestic security alert. Images of the unidentified male thief will be attached to T.V. broadcasts in hopes that someone will come forward with a lead. Absolutely no mention of nuclear materials will leave this office as yet."

Jacinta looked her team over as she finished bringing them up to speed on the events at the nuclear plant. There was silence among the group as they all struggled to take in the video footage Lindel had just played for them.

It was a long moment before Mike looked up with the subconscious frown he subconsciously took on when deeply immersed in his own thoughts.

"Lindel, you'd know better than I," he said. "But aside from the apparent impossibility of what we've just seen, how would one accomplish moving matter through a solid object like this? I mean, science-fiction has been talking about phase shifting and matter displacement for years. In a more practical sense though, humankind is just not that close to having the effective, functional understanding of physics to do such things, are we?"

"If you'd asked me an hour ago, I would have answered with a categorical 'no'," Lindel replied. "To the best of my knowledge we're a long way off that kind of practical application. Why, what are you thinking?"

"So, years away then?" Mike continued, motioning that he would answer in due time.

"Decades. Perhaps centuries," Lindel confirmed.

Mike nodded to himself before continuing. "My point is that a device like this is not just one brilliant discovery away from being created. There would have to be a chain of major breakthroughs and discoveries made over the course of years, which would not necessarily have anything to do with the device itself. Discoveries that would have been major news in the physics world as they came about, and therefore published in numerous scientific journals, government reports, etc. Places where people just such as yourself would no doubt hear about them?"

"That would stand to reason," Lindel confirmed, now frowning as well.

"So where did it come from?" Mike finished, stroking the mousy brown stubble on his chin. "I mean, by necessity most terrorists, thieves, etcetera, employ inferior technology to our own. Some of the most professional outfits have tech equal to the equipment we use. None of the groups we've ever dealt with or even heard about have equipment this far advanced. In fact, to the best of our collective knowledge, no one on earth should, or can, have the theoretical knowledge to construct such a device at this time."

"You'd better not be about to tell me this thing doesn't come from Earth," Jacinta told him seriously.

"Strange things might be happening in this city, but Victoria is clearly human; the man on the reactor footage is as well. Just because we don't comprehend their technology doesn't mean they're from outer space."

"Wait a minute," Andrea interrupted. "What does Victoria have to do with this?"

Jacinta opened her mouth to answer, then closed it again when she realised she didn't have a solid link.

"They both seem to have the ability to make local security feeds go offline," Seth offered. "And they both have knowledge of technology we don't understand. That is, if Victoria's custom parts do indeed belong to a device."

"It is plausible that the two might be linked," Mike added.

"Andrea, check the thief's face against the awakened's files," Jacinta ordered abruptly.

"Lindel, you said that the parts Victoria ordered could be the first stages in some kind of huge cannon. Could they be planning to use the nuclear rods as a power source?"

"I said that was one possibility," Lindel replied. "There are many others equally as valid."

She thought for a long moment before speaking again.

"If it was some form of cannon, it would have to be light, or energy-based to be powered by the nuclear rods. Laser or super-heated plasma most likely. The technology to effectively build such a large-scale weapon of that nature is perhaps a decade away, but not currently within our reach. Of that much I am certain due to various projects I've worked on both for our own government and our allies."

Andrea's computer chimed and her eyebrow rose at the result.

"His name is Marcus Flannigan, thirty-six, resident of Perth. He was a coma patient at Bellmore hospital until he woke at the same time as all the others. Current whereabouts; listed as missing by his wife six days ago…"

Jacinta slowly unclenched the fists she'd made as Andrea delivered her report, and somehow managed not to pound the table in frustration.

"I want a full rundown on each and every awakened across the country. Include financials and current whereabouts for both them and their families since the day they woke until now. Get started and I'll brief Jeff and have him assign more resources."

* * *

8:17

"All right, show me what you've found," Director Illum ordered an hour later as he strode up to Jacinta's desk.

Jacinta's team had been working through the list of awakened patients, with help from the floor, after she'd filled Jeff in on Marcus' identity. They were about four fifths of the way through.

"Nothing good," Jacinta replied as she motioned him to take a seat. "We can confirm so far that ninety-three of the two hundred and eight awakened patients are not where we expected them to be. As of this morning, twenty-nine have been reported missing across various states, another thirty-six have booked holidays by themselves and left in the last few days. We're still trying to confirm they are where they say they are. The remaining twenty-eight seem to have just disappeared."

"What do you mean by disappeared?" Jeff asked.

"Well, not literally of course. They all just seem to have packed up and left. We're tracking what licence plates and bank cards we have, but several patients were in comas for years, and no longer have any such assets. It's making them exceedingly difficult to track."

Jeff's brow furrowed in thought. "Statistically, there's no way this many disappearances in this short a timeframe can be isolated events. What evidence do we have linking the patients between the time of their release from custody and now?"

"None, we've been checking for that as we go. There hasn't been a single point of contact between any of them so far. Which in itself seems strange since we confined groups of them together in various facilities for several weeks. You would think that one of them, somewhere, would have made a friend. The most telling part though is that there is a definite correlation between their actions. The ones who have booked holidays almost all have family ties in their city of residence, those who do not are predominantly the cases of disappearance."

"I'm not sure I like where you're going with this Jacinta."

"Neither am I, Jeff. If we find evidence that these absences can't be explained away as a wild skewing of probability, it points to a massive conspiracy amongst the awakened. Given that at least some of them seem to have gained, through unknown means, technological expertise decades ahead of our own, this problem could be a lot bigger than even I thought."

"What about their financials?" Jeff asked after a moment.

"The analysts are still going through it, but we're getting some rather strange hits."

8:17

"Such as?" Jeff prompted as Jacinta scanned the results the analysts were updating for her in real time.

"We've found fourteen awakened so far, all without family, who have sold their houses in the last two months. Over a dozen book deals and multiple T.V. appearances have been booked by various awakened, yet none of them seem to have an excess of cash in their accounts. In fact they seem to average less than a thousand dollars apiece."

"So where's the money going?" Jeff mused. "As far as we could determine in the initial investigation, for the most part, these are ordinary people with ordinary lives. Very few of them were particularly wealthy or powerful. If our premise of there being a conspiracy is correct, perhaps they are pooling what resources they have in order to achieve a central goal."

"That would make sense actually," Jacinta agreed. "Those parts Victoria ordered from Harberg Fabrications weren't cheap, but we couldn't find a money trail to give us a lead on her finances. If these other awakened were funnelling their own personal fortunes into the project, whatever it is, it would explain a great deal."

Jacinta picked up the phone on the desk they were standing at and dialled Lindel's desk.

"Harding," the woman replied almost instantly.

"Lindel, check the timelines for the major financial windfalls the awakened have come into against the parts orders Victoria placed with Harberg Fabrications please."

"One moment," came the response, then a lengthy delay.

"This is not good," Lindel said a few moments later. "The amounts match up with a reasonable consistency. If I'm interpreting this correctly, each time the collective awakened's finances have reached a critical point, another parts order has ensued within a day. You wanted proof of a conspiracy; I'd say this puts it beyond any doubt."

"Thank you Lindel," Jacinta answered before hanging up.

"You were right," she told Jeff. "But what's their next step? We know they need several more parts to complete whatever this is, but they have to know that these windfalls can't continue indefinitely."

"They'll need more money," Jeff said with a slight smile. "Notify every bank and cash depository in the city and tell them to post guards both inside and outside their vaults."

"Right," Jacinta agreed. "What pretext should we

use for telling them to place guards inside the vaults?"

Jeff thought for a moment.

"Tell them we've received a tip about a group of thieves using high tech laser drilling equipment to come up from underneath. Make it clear to them that any breaches are to be reported immediately, not covered up to save face."

"Done," Jacinta replied as she started moving off.

Jeff picked up the desk phone again and speed dialled Jameson. "I need you to round up a number of the awakened, get the details from Lindel as to specific individuals we have evidence against."

* * *

Two days had passed since he'd given the order to start rounding up the awakened again. Since that time, it felt as though he had spent more hours being raked over the coals by various politicians for not consulting them first, than he had conducting the business of the A.T.U. It had culminated in the Prime Minister's demand that he fly to Canberra to explain his actions in person. Under those orders, Jameson's team, and others around the country, had rounded up nearly fifty of the awakened before the rest of the group had scattered. The carefully planned and coordinated strikes somehow failing to gather in many of their targets, for which he was now also in trouble. He'd gotten out of the meeting with the PM with his job just barely intact. Partly because of the authoritative brief he'd prepared in response, but also because during the interview they'd received news that several tonnes of rare metals had disappeared under mysterious circumstances. It had been a coordinated strike on several government facilities around the country, each baring the hallmarks of the awakened's newfound technological superiority. Only a handful of culprits had been identified during the raids. However, those who had were all on the list the A.T.U. had developed of awakened who had picked up and left their lives under cryptic circumstances. The PM had been less than impressed, but with Jeff's prescient briefing literally in his hand he could hardly condemn the man for not doing his job.

"Jeff."

"What have you got for me Jacinta?" he asked as he looked up from his work screen and saw her standing at the door of his office.

"Victoria, on line two. She somehow managed to call my desk extension direct, then tells me she'll only speak to you."

He couldn't help but stare nonplussed at Jacinta for a moment. She was clearly not impressed at being toyed with by the wanted woman.

"You're kidding," he replied as he pressed the buttons for line two and speaker on the supposedly secure system. By now, a trace would already be well under way.

"Victoria, I hear you'd like to chat," he said in as casual a manner as he could.

"Director Illum, you know who I am, and by now some small part of what we can do. I am calling to request that you cease and desist your persecution of our people. Failure to comply with this most civil request will lead to severe and lethal consequences for a great many people."

"Other than threats, can you give me a particularly compelling reason why I should?" He returned in a falsely jovial tone. "We've already captured over fifty of your people, it's just a matter of time until we round up the rest now that you've confirmed you're all in this together."

"For the sake of brevity I will assume you're tracing this call Director Illum. Understand that when you are able to locate its source, you will better understand the depth of your predicament. I do not lie when I say that millions will be killed if we do not achieve our goals. I also do not lie when I say that even if we succeed, that is perhaps the best possible outcome. There are many other scenarios which end far worse for both your country, and this entire world."

"See. Now I know you're bluffing," he replied. "Even with your newfound technological skills, you don't have the numbers or materials needed to launch an attack on a global scale. You must understand that even if you succeed in whatever it is you're planning, you simply do not have the physical manpower to destroy us."

"You are correct of course, Director Illum, nor would we wish to. In fact I would even go so far as to guarantee you will not be destroyed, so long as you allow us to complete our work."

"What's that supposed to mean?" Illum asked to a suddenly quiet line.

"Trace this call Director Illum, and leave us be."

There was a noise on the other end of the line as though the phone had been knocked. A door closed loudly in the background.

"Hello. Victoria, are you still there?"

He looked over to where Jacinta was still waiting, listening to their conversation. She held up her hands in confusion before calling out.

8:17

"The line's still active, we have a trace. It's in the city."

"Take two teams and investigate," Jeff ordered. "But exercise extreme caution on site, this stinks of a setup."

* * *

A pair of featureless black A.T.U. armoured cars pulled up around the corner from the building the trace had identified. Jameson's men wasted no time exiting the vehicles, taking up the positions he indicated. Seeing that there was no immediate opposition, he signalled two of his soldiers to move up to higher ground as Jacinta and Lindel came up behind him. She had wanted to lead the assault herself, but he'd been able to convince her otherwise. This was, after all, his area of expertise.

He peeked around the corner and spied the alleyway which ran behind the derelict factory, everything looked as it should. So far so good.

"Overwatch to team leader, no movement, thermal's clear," a voice said over his headset a few moments later.

Risking another look, Jameson confirmed the report and made his decision.

"Team one and two, take up assault positions on my mark. Team two has the back, team one with me, overwatch to provide cover as needed. Lethal force is not authorised unless absolutely necessary, we are here for prisoners and intel."

He took a deep breath in preparation for what was to come.

"Mark," Jameson said, and began to move.

With his team behind him and sniper support from the roof, Jameson headed out into the open space of the street. He stretched every sense to capacity in the hope that if something went wrong, his men would have a fraction of a second more to find cover. A few seconds later though they were lined up hard against the front wall of the building without incident, while team two headed around the back, equally unchallenged.

The man behind him wasted no time attaching a small C4 charge to the door lock before getting back into position while Jameson covered the door. A double click on the radio told him team two had done the same.

"Breach on my mark." Jameson said over his radio. "Mark."

The man with the trigger detonated the tiny charge and a similar noise came from round the back. Before the minor explosion had properly cleared, Jameson was through the door and scanning the room as his men fanned out behind him. As per the briefing he'd conducted enroute, his men split up into teams of two. Two pairs would stay on this level to secure the exits while he and another pair headed for the staircase to the left of the entrance. According to Dr. Harding, the trace had indicated a land line on the second floor, not too far from the top of the stairs he was now on. So far there was no sound of gunfire or shouting, which was a good sign. After what he'd seen at the nuclear plant though he wasn't going to rule anything out. After a glance down the second storey corridor, he led his men out as quietly as he could. They passed the open door to an abandoned office, but after clearing it, continued on. The next door was locked, and the third door up ahead was their target. Jameson motioned his men to cautiously pass by the locked room for the moment, choosing to preserve whatever element of stealth remained to them as they approached the closed door.

He put his hand on the doorknob for an instant, and feeling it was cold to the touch, tried turning it as quietly as he could. Surprisingly, it was unlocked. With a nod back to his men he pushed through into the room, weapon raised. His men filed in behind him, ready to confront whoever might be inside in case he fell to enemy fire. Thankfully it was unnecessary.

Inside was a bare room, its only feature, a large dirty window in the far wall. Copious amounts of paint were peeling off the featureless walls, and the room looked as though it hadn't been used in decades. In its centre, however, was a single oddity. A small table, clearly new, had been placed. A cord running to an old landline socket ran between it and a nearby wall. At the table end the cord was plugged into... something. It was pyramidal in nature, and clearly some kind of device. It was also unlike anything he had seen before, which was saying something as the A.T.U. had access to all the latest comm. gear.

"Objective secure," he said over the radio. "Team two, any hostiles?"

"Negative sir, finishing sweep and linking up with your team now, nothing to report."

"All right, secure the exits and send someone to escort Robins and Harding inside, but wait for my all clear to bring them upstairs. We've got something they're going to want to see."

Jameson motioned for his men to continue searching the last two rooms. A few seconds later the sound of the locked door being kicked down reached them, and someone called that it was clear.

8:17

"All clear," Jameson confirmed over the radio. "Bring them up."

A minute later one of his men led Jacinta and Dr. Harding into the room. Dr. Harding wasted no time walking straight to the device to begin her examination.

"What is it?" Jacinta asked after a long moment, her patience wearing thin.

"I don't know," Harding said with a slight frown. "The design is unfamiliar. Best guess, some kind of router. Though the fact that there is only the one cord linking it to the phone line suggests it has an internal power source. There also doesn't appear to be a speaker of any kind. I doubt this is where the call originated, it appears the device is capable of sending and receiving signals wirelessly."

"That doesn't make any sense," Jacinta answered. "If it can communicate wirelessly, why plug it into the landline?"

"At a guess, I'd have to say Victoria was doing her best to make it easy to locate."

"So if the call didn't originate here, where is Victoria?" Jacinta asked.

"I have no way of knowing that until I analyse this device in far more detail," Harding replied.

"I'll need to bring it back with us. If it uses satellite relays as I suspect, I can track the signal back to the appropriate satellite. Once I access the data, I should be able to locate a point of origin for her call. If I can crack its code."

"Really?" Jameson asked, more than a little impressed.

"You have a particular skill set Lieutenant, so do I. The A.T.U. employs each of us for good reason."

"Yes ma'am," Jameson responded with a slight smile.

"If you two are finished?" Jacinta asked. "Threat assessment?"

"Unknown. Definitely recommend quarantine, both physical, and EM during testing," Lindel said without hesitation.

"Undetermined. We need to scan it for traces of explosives before it goes anywhere, but also necessary to mission completion," Jameson added.

"Agreed," Jacinta confirmed. "Lindel, Jameson, package this thing up however you see fit to ensure both its and our safe transit."

"I'll need some things from the cars," Lindel responded. "I could use a little help."

"You two," Jameson motioned for two of his men to escort Lindel out, which they did without a word.

8:17

Once the room was clear, Jameson looked at Jacinta for a long moment while he thought. "The thing I don't understand is why we're here. If Victoria was never actually at these premises, except maybe to drop off this device in person, then this isn't some kind of cat-and-mouse game. She wanted us to find this tech, which doesn't make sense. Why reveal more of their capabilities than they have to? The only other reason I can think of was to lure us into some kind of ambush, but we've found no traps and met no resistance. What's she playing at?"

"Something far more worrying," Jacinta said after a moment.

"What's that?"

"The truth," Jacinta responded at length. "I have a feeling we're not going to like whatever Lindel pulls off that thing one bit."

* * *

Jacinta was sitting at her desk when she saw Lindel lean back in her chair, rub her eyes, and sigh. She was about to tell the analyst to take a break when their eyes met.

"Got it," Lindel said with a tired smile.

She'd been working non-stop on cracking the code from Victoria's device for almost a week now, and they'd pulled in two dozen more of the awakened in the meantime. That still left over a hundred on the loose.

Jacinta hurried over to Lindel's station to see a mass of code scrolling down the screen.

"I thought you said you'd got it?" Jacinta asked after a moment of watching the illegible symbols march by.

Lindel just raised an eyebrow. "I did, it's no longer encrypted. Now I just need to figure out what all this data is."

"We can work on that later; all I need right now is the location Victoria was transmitting from."

Lindel nodded. "Let me see what I can do."

For a long minute she worked on the code, doing only God and maybe three other people on the planet knew what to the data until she eventually shook her head and began again.

"That can't be right," she muttered as she finished again, before running the numbers a third time.

"What's happening Lindel," Jacinta asked, a small, heavy pit settling into the bottom of her stomach.

Lindel looked up with a perplexed expression. "Wait a minute."

8:17

She slid across to a second screen and began pulling up communications satellite positions, then winding them back to the time of the call. She then added military and private satellites until there was a myriad of small red, blue, and green dots encompassing the globe.

"Jacinta, get me N.A.S.A. on the line please."

Seeing a good deal of Lindel's already pale complexion had faded away, Jacinta was disinclined to argue despite the space agency not falling under Australia's political umbrella.

"I'll have to clear that with Jeff."

"Sooner rather than later please," Lindel quietly affirmed.

Walking a little faster than normal, Jacinta entered Director Illum's office and filled him in on the situation.

"I'm not sure what she's found, but she's deeply worried about something," Jacinta finished in a rush.

"All right, head back down and I'll make arrangements to have the call routed to her station," Jeff agreed.

It was almost an hour later when the phone rang at Lindel's desk, and Jacinta motioned to put it on speaker.

"Doctor Harding?" an authoritative voice asked over the line.

"Yes, I'm here with Senior Agent Robbins," she replied tensely.

"My name is Doctor Raynolds," the man replied crisply. "I've been asked by my director to assist you in whatever way I can. So what is it you need today Doctor Harding?"

"I have a signal I'm trying to track, and the readings I'm getting don't make any sense. Can you scan the satellite grid for time index fourteen thirty-three, seventeen seconds GMT at co-ordinates zero-one-three-four-eight-six by two-nine-nine-one-three-five. I need to know if there was anything in a direct altitudinal line at that moment."

"Ok, hold on one minute," Raynolds said absently, the sound of typing replacing his voice over the speaker.

"What's going on Lindel?" Jacinta asked pointedly as Raynolds researched the information she'd requested.

Lindel looked up at her, nervously tapping her fingers on the table. It wasn't something the young analyst made a habit of.

"A math error, I hope," She replied vaguely.

"Or?" Jacinta prompted when she once again fell into silent contemplation.

Lindel looked up again, this time giving Jacinta her full attention.

"Do you remember learning in school that people used to think the world was flat, until one day someone proved that it wasn't?"

Jacinta considered Lindel to be a friend more than a colleague, but right now she was getting a little annoyed at the usually practical woman's vague answers.

"Of course. Your point?" She pushed, tired of the evasive responses.

"This is that day, times a hundred," Lindel answered as the speaker crackled back to life.

"I've got nothing at those coordinates at that time index Doctor Harding."

"And you're sure you can see everything? Military and foreign included?"

"Absolutely. We can't always distinguish what we're tracking, but if it's up there, we can see it."

"And there's no chance an object could be out past your scanning range?"

"There's always that possibility in space," Raynolds

replied sceptically. "But it would have to be halfway to the moon for us not to be able to track it from here. Speaking of which..."

There was the sound of typing once again.

"Huh, well look at that," Raynolds said after a moment. "Looks like there was one thing above your coordinates after all."

For a moment Lindel's hand shook as she moved it towards the phone.

"The moon?" she asked, a muscle in her cheek beginning to twitch.

"The moon," Raynolds confirmed.

"Thank you Doctor. We'll be in touch," Lindel said as she pressed the hang-up button with far more care than was warranted.

"Are you trying to tell me Victoria's call came from space?" Jacinta asked, failing to keep the utter disbelief from her voice. "How is that even possible?"

Lindel looked up at her, and when no words came out, she cleared her throat nervously.

"All signals that bounce off the satellite network come from space," she said. "This one just originates a little further out."

8:17

"You can't be serious," Jacinta said as Lindel sat back in her chair, shaken.

"I am," Lindel said slowly. "I just don't know if I believe it."

"But you just said..?"

"I know. But do you want to go upstairs and tell Director Illum that Victoria has access to spaceflight technology advanced enough to reach the *moon*? Let me go over the device again, maybe there's something I missed that can disprove this…"

"How long?"

Lindel shrugged. "It depends. If this is real, then no amount of time will be enough."

Jacinta sighed. "Get started, but keep this to yourself for now. In the meantime I'll have to fill Jeff in on what we've found. One last question, how confident are you that this could be a mistake?"

This time Lindel answered without hesitation.

"I've already verified it three times. If the data weren't so preposterous, I wouldn't be rechecking at all."

"Lovely," Jacinta muttered as she left Lindel to her work.

CHAPTER 8

"You're going to love this," Director Illum said as he approached Jacinta's desk.

She looked up at him expectantly, pushing aside the mound of paperwork that declaring a signal had originated from the moon had generated. Before now she hadn't even known that forms for encounters possibly not of terrestrial origin existed.

"Your young friend Sarah was just picked up by the police in a suburb along the northern beaches thanks to a tip from a local. Looks like your idea of posting her as a missing child paid off Jacinta. Nice work."

"I need to speak to her."

"I thought you might say that, given what you told me before their release. She's being transported here now."

"Where was she picked up, exactly?" Jacinta asked.

"At the Palm Beach waterfront, approximately thirty kilometres north of the city. According to the report she was alone and staring out at the water. After an hour or so, when no adults came to collect her, the lifeguards notified the police, and they recognised her from the bulletin."

"Come with me," Jacinta said as she stood and walked a few steps to Lindel's station. The director raised an amused eyebrow at her tone, but did as she'd requested.

"Lindel, please pull up a satellite feed of Palm Beach, twenty-kilometre radius."

A few moments later Lindel had the image up on screen, and Jeff pointed to a spot on the map.

"Mark that please," Jacinta asked, and Lindel made a small red dot appear at the point Jeff had indicated.

"Now overlay the properties owned or rented by the awakened."

Lindel worked at her keyboard for a moment and two green dots appeared on the screen.

"Too far away," Jacinta mused when it became apparent that none were in walking distance for the young girl.

"Add properties owned or rented by immediate family members."

The number of dots increased by three, and yet still there was nothing close to where Sarah had been found.

"Extended family?" Jacinta tried in frustration. It was becoming the usual sensation for anything to do with this case.

More dots appeared, and yet still none sprang to life within a three-kilometre radius.

"Not every hunch pays off," Jeff said.

"No. We're missing something here," Jacinta insisted.

"Lindel, pull up Sarah's file please."

A photo of the girl appeared a moment later with her understandably short bio scrolled next to it.

"Skip to family, please."

"What are you getting at Jacinta?" Jeff asked.

"She's too young to own property or drive on her own, or even get on a bus alone without drawing concern, if not outright suspicion. So either she's staying in temporary accommodation such as a hotel or motel, which we can likely discount due to the need for both an accompanying adult, and the bulletins we've been plastering across the T.V. Or she's holed up at someone's house she trusts. Probably a family member. Either way we should have enough to start a search."

Jacinta turned back to the bio and began skimming.

8:17

"Father deceased four years ago, mother accounted for since her disappearance and lives in Penrith. Grandparents on mother's side live in Canada, Grandparents on father's side also deceased."

"Check the grandmother's file," Jeff interjected. "There's a twenty-two-year gap between her and her husband's deaths."

Lindel clicked on a link and Sarah's paternal grandmother's bio came up.

"Huh, look at that. Remarried to one Jason Fox at the age of sixty-seven, but didn't take his name. He's still alive," Lindel added as she pulled up his file.

"Add his current address to the map please Lindel," Jacinta requested.

A moment later the map replaced the file picture, and a single blue dot appeared adjacent to the beach.

Jacinta smiled.

"Gotcha. Permission to take a team and investigate?"

"In a moment. Lindel, why didn't this address come up on our initial sweep?" Director Illum asked, visibly annoyed.

Lindel thought for a moment before coming up with the obvious answer.

"Very simply sir, now that Sarah's paternal grandmother is deceased, they are no longer related."

"That's a serious breach in our search protocols, I want it fixed immediately."

"Yes sir, I'll get someone on it straight away."

"Jacinta, take two full teams. If Sarah was in fact hiding at this address, it's possible other awakened are as well. Use the birds, it's only a matter of time until any others who might be holed up in there find out we have Sarah. They'll scatter as soon as they do."

"You got it."

CHAPTER 9

Jameson leapt off the chopper and moved forward as soon as it touched down, his team fanning out behind him on the empty school oval. On his left, the other bird was just landing, the second team dismounting even as it came to a halt. Within seconds, the choppers were airborne again, and Jameson was glad for the close-fitting assault glasses that meant he didn't have to squint against the flying dirt and grass. He signalled the other team to move towards the target. They were three blocks from their objective, and the plan called for each team to take a different route while Jacinta monitored the operation from the air.

As they approached the edge of the oval, a quick check at the corner of the fence line told him that no threat was being offered as yet. His teams moved on as unobtrusively as possible, though cars driving past were slowing to look. With a block to go, the teams split up and Jameson took his men through a private property and over a fence into the yard neighbouring the target property. A fat man in a tattered blue singlet and shorts picked up a meat cleaver from the barbeque he was cooking at. He lowered it slowly again as more of Jameson's men appeared in his yard.

Jameson grimaced and motioned his men to continue to the rally point as he approached the homeowner.

"Agent Jameson, A.T.U. I need you to go inside for your own safety, sir," he said as quickly as possible.

The man just looked at him blankly for a second. "The what? What the blazes is the A.T.U.?"

"Anti-Terrorist Unit," Jameson said brusquely.

"Never heard of it," he replied, though somewhat more cooperatively.

"That's because we're doing our job," Jameson replied. "Now, I need you to go inside, Sir."

"Okay, okay," the man said, throwing his hands up in disgust. "Flamin' terrorists. Getting' to be so that a man can't even enjoy his lunch without hearing about flamin' terrorists anymore."

"Yes, sir," Jameson replied, restraining the grin that tugged at his lips as the man flicked off the gas, hastily loaded the row of barely cooked sausages onto a plate and headed indoors.

8:17

Jameson jogged across the yard and caught up with his team, who were already in position. He took his place at the head of the line and settled in to wait for the signal from team two, who'd been required to traverse a longer route.

"Jacinta, any movement?" he asked over the radio.

"Infrared shows eight people in the house, none in the yard. Three on your side, ground floor, in what appears to be the kitchen, and five in an upstairs room closer to team two's position. It's hard to make out what they're doing, but they seem to be working on something together."

About half a minute later, there was a double squelch on his radio. Jameson looked back at his team to make sure they were ready.

Seeing they were, he pressed the talk button. "Teams in position."

"All teams move in. Good hunting," Jacinta gave the command.

He vaulted the fence as quietly as possible, knowing the other team had heard Jacinta's order over their own headsets and would commence the assault accordingly.

Whether some internal security had been tripped, or ill luck had caused one of the inhabitants to look out a window at the wrong moment was unclear, but a shout went up from inside the house almost immediately. Jameson and the men behind him were forced to sprint for the nearest wall, and the mediocre cover it provided. The rest of the yard was a lawn. As soon as the first of his men reached the wall beside him, he looked back for just a second to confirm the rest were safely on their way. What greeted him was the shocking sight of a bright green beam of light striking Parker in the chest. The man fell soundlessly, and as he came to rest, the reason was clear. Where the man's vital organs should have been was now a gaping hole the size of a dinner plate. The blast had gone straight through his clothing, tactical armour, and even his body, leaving the edges of everything blackened and cauterised as though by fire.

For half a heartbeat Jameson crouched there, completely frozen, until a scream sounded from the other side of the house.

He touched his radio as he shook his head to clear it of the gruesome sight of Parker's mangled body.

"This is Jameson, lethal force is authorised. Grenades and smoke, now."

His unoccupied men pulled their smoke grenades and moved out of the dubious cover of the wall just long enough to throw them at every available window. Hopefully the smoke would buy enough time while their companions dashed across the yard and out of the direct line of fire. Only the team leaders carried frag grenades. Jameson pulled his and threw it through the window of the room where the awakened's shot trajectory said it must have come from on the second floor.

"Cover," he shouted, and his men ducked as debris and glass came exploding out from the section of wall his grenade blew apart.

Before the rain of rubble had even halted, Jameson was up and kicking down the door. He dove to the ground as soon as it swung open and saw a green light flash above him. The man behind him swung his gun around the corner and fired three quick shots. There were no more beams of light, and the soldier moved into the house, followed by the rest of the line as Jameson regained his feet. There was a sudden barrage of gunfire and green light, and Jameson whipped his gun around to see three of his men already down with horrendous wounds. Around another doorway, a man in civilian clothes was aiming some form of weapon at his men. Jameson shot him between the eyes without a second thought.

There was a moment of reprieve, and he tapped his radio.

"Jacinta, how many left?"

"There's three still moving. They've fled upstairs. One is waiting in ambush at the top of the stairs, the other two are trying to carry the one your grenade wounded earlier out a side window."

"Team one and two, hold position," Jameson ordered as he hurried across the room to pick up one of the dead awakened's horrifically powerful weapons.

It was an odd design, and looked to have been cobbled together from random technology rather than manufactured for a purpose. There was a pressure pad replacing a standard trigger mechanism. Still, its operation appeared straightforward enough.

He moved into the hallway and saw where the stairs rose to the next level.

"I need an exact location on the target at the top of the stairs, Jacinta."

"East side, one metre north of the top step on the other side of the dry wall."

"Tell me when I'm right under him," Jameson said as he took a few quiet steps toward where he thought Jacinta had indicated.

"Stop," her voice came through the radio.

He took two steps back, pointed the awakened's weapon at the spot on the roof, and fired.

There was no kick at all, but a vibrant green light sprung out and drilled a two-foot hole in the roof. Jameson fired again, and a third time to be sure. He immediately regretted it as what was left of the awakened's body fell through the now sizable hole in the ceiling. The ruined mass of flesh nearly landed on him in a spray of gore that soured even his battle-hardened stomach.

"Jameson, the remaining three have made it to the lawn. Intercept and take a prisoner."

"I'll do what I can," Jameson replied. "In the meantime, have a bird ready to land in the front yard as soon as we clear the last of the hostiles. We have multiple critical wounded in need of immediate evac."

"Copy that," Jacinta returned after a momentary pause.

"Team two, converge on the west side of the house and take prisoners if possible. If they offer resistance, put them down with overwhelming force. Norrie, stay here and see to the wounded. Benson, Herald, you're with me," he gave his men the commands in swift succession before moving to the front door.

After switching back to his more familiar rifle, he

made a quick check and rounded the corner, only to be greeted by a lance of green light. The shot went well wide as the escaping man who fired it stumbled. Jameson shot the combatant in the arm and the man dropped his weapon with a yell as the others turned to confront his men. Someone from team two shot the second awakened twice as he attempted to raise another of those strangely constructed weapons. Without their support, the companion they'd been trying to aid collapsed to the ground, her leg visibly broken.

"Secure them," Jameson ordered, keeping his weapon trained on the woman whilst Benson and Herald moved in to comply. The man Jameson had shot was unconscious and Benson had no trouble, but as Herald turned the woman over, Jameson abruptly realised who she was.

"Hello Victoria," he said as Herald bound her wrists with a zip tie. "I know someone who would very much like to talk to you."

"Jameson, you've got two more hostiles incoming. They've just appeared in the house and are moving towards you."

There was a flash of green off to the side. One of the men from team two fell to the ground, cut nearly in two by whatever advanced weaponry these awakened had constructed.

8:17

"Cover!" Jameson yelled as a second shot took the arm off another of his men. There was a volley of bullets from the members of his own team, who weren't yet in the line of fire as they shifted position back towards the house. The lone remaining uninjured member of team two joined them, dragging his fallen companion none too gently along with him.

"Jacinta! Where are they coming from?!"

"I don't know... wait, another one just appeared... there must be some kind of shielded bunker beneath the house. You have two hostiles on the outer wall of the kitchen and another circling the house anticlockwise, attempting to flank you."

"Got it. Let me know if any more appear."

He motioned the last remaining member of team two to come closer.

"Carol, I know this is not going how we'd planned, but get Lowrire to the lounge room with the others and place yourself at Norrie's disposal. Protect the wounded at all costs."

The junior member of team two was now their only active member.

"Aye sir," the young man answered in a steadier tone than Jameson would have expected.

"Benson, Herald, with me."

He moved to the nearest corner of the house and waited until he heard footsteps. They were faint, but the lawn was neglected and crunchy. He whipped his gun around the corner and fired the instant the barrel came in line with his target. The woman went down without getting off a shot.

Jameson tapped his radio. "Norrie, I'm going to draw their fire, be ready to take them out from behind."

There was only silence in response.

"Norrie," he tried again.

"Carol here sir. Norrie's dead. They're all dead! The hostiles in the house must have executed them before engaging us again," the young man told him, this time sounding well and truly shaken.

For a long moment Jameson didn't know what to say as he felt his professional detachment shatter.

"Carry out my orders, son," he managed to get out.

"Hostiles are on the move," Jacinta's voice came over the headset. "They're splitting up, one heading to Carol, one to you out the kitchen window."

"Take them out," Jameson told his last remaining men quietly over comms.

8:17

He stooped to pick up a brick that had been knocked loose in the firefight as Benson moved to the corner.

Jameson held up three fingers, then two, and finally one before throwing the brick out past the corner.

A bolt of bright green light turned it into an explosion of dust so quickly it had to have been a reflex shot at the suddenly moving target. Benson leaned around the corner and fired.

"Clear," he said a moment later.

There was a flash inside the house and the sound of gunfire before Carol's shaky voice came over the radio.

"Secure. But I need evac."

"Benson, Herald, clear the house and find out where they were coming from. Jacinta, evac now if your screens are clear."

"Inbound. E.T.A. twenty seconds. Hold on," Jacinta's strained voice came back a moment later.

"Victoria!" Jameson suddenly remembered.

"Chopper two is in pursuit. Clear the house," Jacinta ordered over the radio.

"Acknowledged," Jameson returned as he jogged back to the front of the house and went in search of Carol.

What he found was not good. Carol's leg was missing nearly to the thigh with only a burnt stump remaining. He was barely conscious. Lowrire was not in much better shape, but had held onto his weapon with his one remaining arm, and from their positions, apparently taken out the final assailant himself. Both were in shock, though Carol seemed the worse of the two, and Jameson immediately set about staunching the nearly cauterised wound.

"Chopper's inbound to take you boys home. Hang in there," Jameson hollowly assured them as the noise of the evac chopper grew steadily louder, then became deafening as it touched down on the lawn outside.

A moment later Jacinta hurried into the room, followed by a pair of agents. The trio just stopped, appalled at the sight before them.

"Get these men to the chopper," he barked.

The two agents looked at him numbly for a moment, then hurried to comply. The two men picked Lowrire up first, as he was nearest. Jacinta was forced to step over several body parts to join Jameson and help lift Carol off the floor.

"Don't think about it. Just get them to the chopper," he breathed as she stumbled over somebody's severed and burnt arm.

8:17

As quickly as possible, they hauled the now unconscious Carol to the evacuation chopper. Jameson secured him for flight while Jacinta gave the pilot orders to take them to the nearest hospital. As soon as the four of them were clear, the chopper lifted off.

Jameson suddenly remembered the man he'd shot out on the lawn, and darted around the house to make sure he hadn't escaped.

He was still lying there, unconscious, and Jameson ordered the two agents to take the man into custody.

"I don't understand," Jacinta commented. "None of the other awakened we've arrested has offered lethal resistance. Why here? Why now?"

"I don't know," Jameson replied, hands shaking as the adrenaline which had soaked his system during the short but bloody battle wore off. "But we were not ready, and it's cost us badly. I came in here with twelve men. I've got three left, including myself, and two others who are maimed for life. And for what?"

Jacinta put a hand on his shoulder and then turned away as Benson exited the house and headed toward them.

"Let's find out," she told him as he took a deep breath before turning back towards Benson to hear his report.

"Ma'am," Benson acknowledged Agent Robbins. "Sir, the house is clear, but there's something you both need to see."

"What did you find?" Jacinta asked as she wasted no time moving back towards the house.

"Not my field of expertise, ma'am. But they fought real hard to protect it."

In silent agreement, they entered the house through the back door to avoid the horrific scene in the lounge room. Benson led them through to the kitchen where a section of floor tiles had been peeled back to reveal a hidden basement entrance which Herald was guarding.

"Chopper two, suspect is in custody," a voice came over the headset.

"Good work, chopper two," Jacinta acknowledged. "Bring her back to the house and escort her to the basement, then take custody of the second prisoner. Relay to Director Illum that we need a full containment unit here immediately."

"Acknowledged," came the response.

Jacinta returned her attention to them, and Jameson motioned Herald to lead the way.

"Benson, wait up here and escort Victoria down when she arrives."

"Yes, sir," he responded sharply before heading back to the lawn.

By then Herald was descending the metal rungs of the makeshift ladder. Jameson motioned her to follow.

*   *   *

Jacinta headed down the shaft and found that it was deeper than she'd expected.

"How far down does this go, Sergeant?" She asked after about the thirtieth rung.

"About fifty feet, ma'am. I'm at the bottom now."

She continued for another few moments as Jameson entered the tunnel above her and began his own descent.

Abruptly, her foot hit the ground instead of another rung, and Jacinta stepped off the ladder. She turned to find Herald standing a few feet away, covering the huge room with his upraised weapon. It was probably unnecessary, but they'd already been ambushed once by the awakened waiting in this cavern, undetected and unanticipated until they'd boiled out into the house above.

Jacinta turned around and couldn't help but stare in

awe at the sheer scope of the… thing, before her.

"What the blazes..." she heard Jameson mutter as he exited the ladder and came to stand beside her.

Jacinta took a moment more to respond, still trying to wrap her mind around the sheer size of the construction the awakened had been undertaking down here.

"Herald, get Ms. Harding please," she forced herself to say.

With only the quickest glance to see if Jameson approved, Herald slung his weapon and returned to the surface.

"That housing is definitely the last order Victoria picked up from Harberg Fabrications," Jameson remarked as they studied the fifty-foot-high machine which dominated the open space of the cavern. There were lights of some kind embedded around the walls, but they offered a strange and diffuse glow, and seemed not to be connected to any visible power source.

"Whatever this thing is, we didn't give them time to finish it at least."

Jacinta couldn't help but notice the open panels as she took a few steps toward the base of the huge machine.

"What on earth is this thing?" she muttered, "And how did they excavate this cavern without the neighbours thinking there was an earthquake going on night and day?"

"So, not a modern art project then…" Lindel said a few minutes later as she stepped into the cavern and examined the machine before them, her expert eye taking in every detail.

"What is it?" Jacinta felt the sudden need to ask, even though she knew the analyst had no way of answering just yet.

Lindel just looked at her for a moment, then back at the mammoth machine.

"Well, at first glance, it is a complex system judging from the swivel base and armature at the balance point. The aperture at the apex has what appears to be one hundred and eighty degrees of spherical line-of-sight possibilities. Much like a satellite dish," she added when Jameson gave her a questioning look.

"Why would anyone put a satellite dish underground?" Jacinta asked, not sure she was following Lindel's train of thought.

"They wouldn't," she replied whilst examining the ground around the machine. "In addition, there is no lift system built into this room, meaning that whatever its function, it was meant to be carried out right here."

"Underground?" Jameson asked, his face turning a slight shade of green.

"What's wrong?" Lindel asked, taking hold of the big man's arm to steady him. Jameson looked as though he might lose his lunch right there.

In a heartbeat Jacinta was at his side as well, but Jameson waved them off as he regained some of his colour. He slowly pulled the awakened's pistol from his belt.

"No…" Jacinta muttered, horrified at the very thought of what Jameson was proposing. She'd seen the carnage which that makeshift, and yet handheld weapon had caused in the house above.

If Jameson were right...

"I don't understand?" Lindel replied, her gaze flitting from Jameson's sickened expression to Jacinta's horrified one and back again.

"Show her," Jacinta ordered as she pointed to a section of wall well away from the tunnel to the surface.

Jameson opened his mouth as if to say something, then shut it again with a frown of grim determination. He levelled the weapon at the area Jacinta had indicated before squeezing the grip.

8:17

There was no sound, no recoil, just a blaze of green light that seemed to pass straight into the wall. Lindel jumped at the unexpected weapon fire, but pulled herself together quickly. With an almost offended frown, she went to inspect the clean, circular hole the weapon fire had left in the bedrock.

She pulled a small LED torch from a pocket and shone it down the hole before turning back with a daunted look on her face.

"Who *are* these people?" she whispered, before panicking and rushing over to the open console the awakened had not been given time to complete. With a frown, she pushed aside a bundle of wiring and examined where the connections led.

"What's going on?" Jacinta called after a moment, receiving no response.

Looking at the base of the console, Lindel traced a conduit around to the far side of the hulking machine. After two steps, she backed away with a horrified expression of her own.

"Get out," she called in escalating panic. "Get out right now!"

"Go!" Jameson yelled at a startled Jacinta as he raised the awakened's weapon in response.

"That won't help," Lindel shouted as she sprinted

past him and began to climb. Jacinta was a heartbeat behind her after waiting just long enough to ensure Lindel was safely away before she began her own ascent.

* * *

Jameson tucked the weapon away as he backed towards the tunnel and began taking the rungs two at a time, taking Lindel's warning to heart. By the time he reached the surface, Lindel was already racing towards her gear while Jacinta, seemingly on Lindel's orders, was ordering a full evacuation of the premises. A moment later, Lindel came dashing back to them, Benson in tow, a horrifying piece of equipment held in her hand. She scanned each of the four team members who had been in the cavern intently, including herself, before putting the Geiger counter down on the grass with badly shaking hands.

"We're okay..." she told them, trembling, while Jacinta paled in sudden realisation of where this was heading. "But whatever that thing down there's purpose is, it's powered by four of our missing nuclear fuel rods."

CHAPTER 10

"You're going to love this," Seth Gabel, their resident expert in languages announced as he walked up to Jacinta's desk. In his hand he clutched a file which he placed in front of her with a smug grin.

"You know, people keep saying that, and it never turns out to be true."

She opened the folder anyway and began to read.

"What is wrong with these people?" Jacinta muttered as she slammed the folder closed again.

"Does Jeff know yet?"

Seth shook his head. "Not yet. Only just confirmed it a moment ago."

"Come with me," Jacinta ordered as she stood and led the way to the A.T.U. director's office.

"Lindel won't be happy," Seth commented as they walked.

"Perhaps not. But I'm ecstatic," Jacinta replied.

"This is the best news we've had since those people woke up.

Once they reached the upper floor, and the office which overlooked the rest of the workspace, Jacinta knocked and waited until Director Illum called for them to enter.

"What have you got?" he asked as soon as the door sealed closed behind them.

"I'll let Seth fill you in on this one," Jacinta replied, nodding towards the red-haired analyst beside her.

For a moment Seth seemed surprised, but recovered quickly.

"Okay, the short version is that the signal device we recovered from Victoria's safe house, the one which relayed the transmission from the moon, is a fraud."

"In what way?" Director Illum demanded. "I thought Lindel went over that thing with a fine-toothed comb?"

"She did," Seth acknowledged. "She ran every test in the book and then some. Unfortunately, the book hasn't really helped us all that much with this case so far, Sir."

"That's the truth," Director Illum muttered. "Are you now telling me that Victoria and her people do not, in fact, have access to space flight capabilities?"

"I can't speak to that, Sir. But there is no longer any reason to believe they do so because of device we recovered."

"I see. Well, that's good enough for now, I guess. Give me the details."

Seth frowned in thought.

"Lindel's tests all ran true, Sir, but I just didn't believe it. The fact is that regardless of where they've acquired this extra knowledge, these people aren't from the future, and they're not aliens. They're just people, born and raised right here in this country and others just like it. We have their birth records, schools they attended, family histories and more. I simply didn't buy that they could have gathered the knowledge to design and build a space borne signal relay. Not to mention having the means of getting it out of low orbit and all the way to the moon without a single space agency worldwide tracking the launch or lunar approach. On the premise that this meant the device absolutely had to be a hoax, I dug into its programming extensively and found, well, nothing amiss. All of which mirrored Ms. Harding's findings."

Seth stopped to clear his throat. "I'll save you most of the technical details, but the programming appears legitimate. With a proper transmitter, I believe it could actually do what it was pretending to, which is why the device is so convincing. At any rate, I was able to determine that the amount of data storage on the hard drive was very slightly off from what the device was claiming. That's when I began to see what had been done. With that lead, I filled up the drive with rubbish information until it was maxed out. Then I used a tracker program to monitor which sectors were left out when I erased that same information. This gave me a map of sorts as to where to look for the concealed files. There were several other steps, but you get the idea. Eventually I was able to piece together the remains of a minute program, one isolated from the main platform, which is why Lindel's tests never detected it. Essentially, this small program was the only genuine thing on the drive. As far as I can determine, it only did two things, and had a self-delete function which kicked in once those tasks were complete. First, it routed the call from a number which is registered to the house we raided yesterday, to us. The time stamp matches Victoria's call. Second, it fooled the main platform itself into thinking the call was originating from the coordinates Lindel found. That's why she couldn't determine that they were altered. The very program she was investigating was also being fooled into thinking they were legitimate."

There was a long moment of silence as Seth finished

his explanation, and by now Jeff was frowning deeply.

"And you're sure about this?"

"Yes Sir," Seth replied. "I reactivated the hidden program and tested it with several locational coordinates. The results were consistent that the main program was fooled into thinking the coordinates were legitimate in each case. Examination of the new data within the program failed to turn up any trace of tampering."

"That's excellent work, Mr. Gabel," the director told him. "Now if you two will please excuse me, I have an uncomfortable call to make to the Prime Minister."

Before he could say anything else, the phone on his desk rang. Jeff picked it up as the others turned to leave.

"You're sure?" he asked in a tone that caused Jacinta to stop at the door and pay attention.

"Very well, isolate it and I'll have our techs there in a few hours."

Hanging up the phone, Jeff scowled for an instant.

"Seth, find Lindel and get a team ready. Our operatives in Perth have found another one of these machines, along with four more of the missing fuel rods, and this one is complete. Jacinta, I want you to interrogate Victoria again. I doubt she'll give us anything, but see what you can do with this new information. If that doesn't yield any results, take another run at Sarah. Maybe she'll be a little more cooperative."

"I think I may have an idea about that, Sir," Jacinta acknowledged in sudden thought.

"Good," Jeff barked. "I'm sick of not knowing what's happening with these people. We've recovered eight fuel rods, but that still leaves forty unaccounted for. That's up to ten more of these machines they're willing to kill and die to protect in undisclosed locations. And if the one in Perth is indeed complete…"

"Then others won't be far behind," Jacinta finished.

"Or are already built," Jeff amended. "And once they are, the awakened could activate them at any moment. We're running out of time, Jacinta. Find me some answers."

"Yes Sir," Jacinta replied before leaving the office and heading back down to the main floor.

"What do you need?" Seth asked as they returned to their work area.

Jacinta just looked at him for a moment. "Just do

what the director told you. Take Lindel and get to Perth. Find out what these things are, because even if Victoria does answer my questions, I don't want to be forced to take her word for it."

*   *   *

Minutes later, Jacinta had reached the interrogation area and headed down the hallway to room three, where Victoria was being held. She entered the doorway to the adjacent monitoring room and nodded to the technician who was staring at the displays, which were currently assessing the prisoner. There was no window in this cell, no double-sided glass, only four concrete walls along with a floor and ceiling of exactly the same dimensions, forming a perfect cube. Located deep within the recesses of the building, when the lights were off as they were now, the cell was a perfect pitch black. Added to this, the entire room was soundproofed to make a sort of sensory deprivation cell. The monotony was broken only by a myriad of sensors built into covered crevasses in the walls. Jacinta had sat in there herself when the room had first been built, and she'd been desperate to get out by the time an hour had passed. Victoria had been in there for nearly two days so far, but had yet to show a single sign of impatience.

Jacinta thought for a moment about how to approach the woman now that her bluff with the transmission had been revealed. There was a fine line to be walked here. Push too hard and Victoria would stop talking as she had in each of their previous sessions. On the other hand, to not push hard enough was to waste time and effort for no payoff. She would have to approach this carefully.

"When was the last time she slept?" she asked the tech.

The unfamiliar man checked a clipboard next to him before answering.

"From three thirty-six a.m. to eleven nineteen," he said in a bored tone.

Nearly four hours ago, Jacinta thought to herself.

Good.

"In a moment, I want you to flood the room with as much illumination and noise as possible. Keep it going until I'm seated and then drop the lights to normal and cut the sound as abruptly as you can. Make sure every device you've got is recording the session. I'll need it later."

"You got it," the tech replied.

On the monitor in front of her, Victoria was sitting in a relaxed position, despite her wrist being bound to the tabletop by a short cord. Her sense of ease annoyed Jacinta for some deep-seated reason.

"Okay. Hit it," Jacinta told the tech. She couldn't help a satisfied smirk when Victoria startled enough at the abrupt onslaught that she nearly fell off her chair, clutching at her eyes and ears in a futile attempt to mitigate the sudden, blinding cacophony assaulting her senses.

Jacinta slipped through the adjoining door without hesitation, closing it behind her and seating herself in the chair opposite Victoria without undue fuss. Once she was in position, the ear piercingly loud shrieking halted mid wail, and the lights returned to normal.

She sat there silently as Victoria recovered and noticed her with a start.

"Thank you for that," Victoria acidly remarked. "Am I supposed to be impressed by that entrance?"

Jacinta let out a small laugh.

"Entrance? I've been here for hours. Since before you woke up in fact."

Victoria gave her a flat look. "I would have heard you breathing."

"Yes, of course you would." Jacinta replied with a small, knowing smirk that seemed to have the desired effect.

"What do you want this time?" Victoria asked, attempting to steer the conversation back to more comfortable ground.

"Oh, not much. Actually, I came to give *you* some information," Jacinta replied in a conspiratorial tone.

"Really?" Victoria replied in mock earnestness. "Please, do tell."

"Okay," Jacinta told her, leaning in as though not to be overheard. "We found another one of your machines. It was finished this time, so Lindel thinks she'll be able to work out what it does pretty quickly."

Victoria leaned back with a satisfied grin.

"Only one?"

"So far. But now that we know how your people are operating, we're confident the others won't remain hidden much longer. So I was wondering, what would happen if we did find them all?" Jacinta asked casually. "Would that worry you?"

"Of course," Victoria replied, giving an uncharacteristically straight answer.

"Why?" Jacinta replied, hoping she wasn't taking this line too far.

"We'll need them soon."

"I see. To complete your mission?"

"Yes. It goes without saying that the more of them we have online, the better our chances will be."

"So you don't think you'll need them all, then?" Jacinta remarked, filing that bit of information away for later.

For a moment Victoria's mouth thinned and Jacinta realised she was about to clam up again.

"Well, that's about it for now," Jacinta said as she stood and took a few steps towards the door.

"Oh, wait," she remarked as she turned again to face the prisoner.

"I almost forgot to tell you; we deconstructed your device. The transmission came from your safe house, not the moon. You didn't really think we would buy that, did you?"

Victoria shrugged. "It amused me to think that you might," she admitted. "But in the end, it was never meant to be more than a simple bit of theatre to keep you chasing your tails while my people worked."

"Don't suppose you want to save some time and tell me what this super-secret mission of yours is? I mean, it's only a matter of time until we figure it out ourselves now that we have one of your completed machines in our custody. You do realise that once that happens, you will have nothing left to bargain with, don't you?"

"Why would I need to bargain?" Victoria asked with a raised eyebrow.

For a moment, her easy response stopped Jacinta in her tracks.

"No matter what you do. No matter whether we succeed. Very soon I will no longer be in your custody. And Jacinta, there is nothing on this world that will help you find me once I'm gone."

"Just on this world?" Jacinta asked innocently.

Victoria blinked. "You have a way of twisting words to your advantage Jacinta. I misspoke of course. After all, it's not like I come from the moon, now is it?"

Jacinta tried a different tack. "See, here's the thing I can't work out. If your people are this intent on building these nuclear-powered weapons and defending them to the death, what are you after? I mean, you can't honestly think we'll pay you some form of ransom. All your associates are known and will eventually be rooted out, so completing your mission and disappearing is out of the question. Add the fact that now that we know how you're operating, we'll find your other machines soon enough, meaning time becomes an issue for your people. So what is it, Victoria? What's so important to all of you that returning to your lives is now forever out of the question? That you don't even hesitate at dying in the completion of your goals. What's the end game?"

For a long moment Victoria studied her without speaking, until with a small crease of her brow, she cocked her head.

"All right, I'll throw you a bone," she replied. "No matter what you think of what we're doing. Or what orders you have from your superiors. I promise you that the more of our machines you take offline around the world, the worse it will be for all of you when the time comes for them to fulfil their task."

"Who is 'all of you'?" Jacinta asked.

"You," Victoria spoke calmly. "People. Humans."

Jacinta just looked at her for a long moment. Victoria obviously now felt composed enough to play with her, which meant it was time to bring this session to an end.

"Despite the advanced knowledge your people have somehow attained, you're as human as I am," she said in dismissal, turning away.

"Of course I am," Victoria added as Jacinta opened the door to leave. "All the tests say so..."

Jacinta nodded slightly to herself and left a smirking Victoria in her cell.

CHAPTER II

Two car rides and a five-hour plane trip later, Lindel stepped off a makeshift ladder into a cavern much like the one they'd found in Sydney, and followed Seth inside.

His findings on Victoria's signal diverter had been a watershed moment for Lindel. When everybody kept saying you were one of the smartest people in the country, it was apparently enough to make you start believing it. She'd worked on failed projects before, but never one which had faltered due to her own inability to solve a problem. There was no excuse for sloppy work, especially in such a high stakes operation. In truth, she wasn't upset with Seth, his brilliant work had caught and mitigated much of her mistake, and he'd been surprisingly gracious about the whole affair. She was, however, still embarrassed with herself for missing the actual function of the device, resulting in a report detailing a terrorist group's supposed spaceflight capabilities.

A report which had been circulated right up to the Prime Minister's office. In all, it hadn't surprised her when Seth had been chosen to lead this trip. There was obviously still work to be done regaining Director Illum's confidence.

Across the cavern sat a device of identical construction to the one previously uncovered. Only this time the control panels were finished, and the array at its apex appeared to be complete.

A thin man of Japanese descent wearing full tactical gear and a deep scowl abruptly blocked her way.

"I lost a lot of good men here today, Doctor. Make sure it wasn't for nothing," he said in flawless English before allowing her to proceed. She nodded in acknowledgement, unprepared for the sudden encounter. Having read the report on the way over, she knew that the assault on this site had cost even more lives than the one in Sydney. These men had known what they were heading into and come prepared. Yet somehow the awakened had known they were coming, and ambushed them from the rear once the assault had already begun. The team had been caught in a crossfire by the same horrifically powerful weapons they had deployed in the Sydney defence. It was amazing that any of the A.T.U team had survived, let alone been able to complete their mission. Fourteen more of the awakened had been killed in the assault, with two more captured. The prisoners weren't talking yet, or so she'd been told on the way in.

Seth had preceded her to the machine, and she saw his immediate look of concern.

"What is it?" Lindel asked as she approached, but immediately saw the problem.

"You, over here," Lindel called to an agent busy photographing the scene.

The man approached, and she pointed to the console. "Photograph everything here, and send the images to cryptography before you continue with the rest of the scene. Mark them as critical priority, with results to be returned to Dr. Gable."

The man nodded and began documenting the panel from every angle at varying magnifications, then moved away to follow his other instructions.

For a long moment Lindel frowned at the writing, if that's what it was, before glancing towards Seth, who was openly perplexed.

"I don't want to say this," Seth said for her ears only. "But I've spent my entire life studying languages. It's what I do. Modern, ancient, computing, mathematical… This is entirely unfamiliar to me."

He scanned the writing for a moment longer.

"These passages are too long and too few to be a standard letter structure, and I can identify at least forty individual characters just in this first string. None of which repeat. I suppose each one could represent a word, or a sound even. Maybe each string represents a sentence or paragraph? Though if that were the case, there should be at least some repetition."

"Common words like 'the' or 'it'?" Lindel asked.

"Exactly."

He spent a moment checking the rest of the panel, glancing over literally hundreds of distinct characters. "There just isn't *any* repetition," he scowled. "Even if this were something vaguely akin to a Mandarin style structure, it would imply the need for literally thousands of characters to make up the language. You would have to learn all of them in order to read it. Not to mention that if the characters do represent individual words, you would need to add new characters to the language all the time. You'd have to disseminate them throughout the population every single time something new was discovered or invented, in any field of interest."

"Could it be some kind of cypher?" Lindel suggested.

"I hope so," Seth replied. "Because if it's not, we'll

never crack it without a keystone. But beyond that…"

"Beyond that," Lindel replied with a vague shudder, "It would be unlike anything else that's been developed during all human history."

Seth nodded.

"Don't tell the others," he eventually managed. "But at this point, I don't mind saying that I'm beginning to get a terrible feeling about where all this is heading."

"Assuming the writing is not just another elaborate distraction, we'll crack it eventually," Lindel tried to assure him.

"No, you're missing the point," Seth insisted. "This can't be a trick. Either the writing is a language or code, or it's gobbledygook. There's no wriggle room for theatrics on this one like there was with the transmitter, no way to fake a language without first creating that language. If all they wanted was to mislead us, they wouldn't go to all that effort, they'd just write the lies down in a recognisable method."

"So, just write 'press the red button' when we actually need to press the green one?"

"Exactly," Seth replied. "But in a language we can read. You just wouldn't go to the ridiculous length of creating an incredibly complex language from scratch for us to find. Especially knowing that we would almost certainly not be able to crack it."

"So assuming it's not just a distraction…?" Lindel asked, wondering where he was heading with his line of thought.

"*If* it's real, the entire world is about to have a far bigger problem than a few unidentifiable machines."

"Bigger than a worldwide conspiracy aimed at building unidentified nuclear-powered devices?" Lindel asked, taken aback.

Seth gave her a guarded look for a long moment.

"Yes," he eventually replied. "I don't want to say anything more at this point as I have only suspicions to put forward. Ones I'm not even sure I believe myself. And no hard evidence to back up any of it that could go into a report. But there's been too much oddness since the awakening, too many things we can't explain. Patterns are starting to form if you know where to look, and I don't like the direction they seem to be pointing. I can't shake the feeling that something big is coming, just over the horizon now, and we're not at all ready for it."

Lindel nodded slowly. She'd been feeling the same way ever since she'd examined Victoria's signal device. Although that machine had turned out to be a fraud, the feeling that many things were subtly wrong about it had never really left. She'd simply never put it into words as clearly as Seth just had.

They shared a glance as she placed a hand on his shoulder.

Seth gave her a tight smile, then turned back to the machine. "We'd better get the equipment set up."

She nodded in agreement.

* * *

It was several hours later when Lindel finally felt comfortable making a conclusion.

"It's definitely an array. The fuel rods are connected to this system, which I can't even begin to identify without taking it apart piece by piece. The power lines lead all the way up these conduits, which after they've passed through several other components, lead to the mouth of the aperture."

"Well, at least now we're sure," Seth replied from underneath the control console where he'd discovered more of the strange writing some time before.

"Anything on your end?" Lindel inquired.

"No. I'm just about ready to give up on this and start on the programming. Have you found anything that looks like an input?"

"Yes, there's a small antenna behind the panel to my left."

Seth looked over to where she was pointing and stiffly got to his feet. He retrieved his laptop from a nearby folding table brought in by their people and began attempting to connect it to the machine.

"Whoa," he exclaimed a moment later.

Lindel looked across at his expression before stepping down from the ladder she was using and walking over to stand behind him.

"What is that?" she asked, as surprised as Seth had been a moment ago.

"I do not know, but it's in the same language as the writing on the console, and there are whole lot more characters than we saw over there."

"So it is a language?" Lindel confirmed.

"Or the most annoying screen saver of all time," Seth remarked with a small grin.

Lindel couldn't help noticing though that Seth looked a little paler than he had a moment ago.

"Let's see what this button does," he said as he

pressed the space key with a half grin and a small shrug, causing the writing to immediately disappear. The abruptness of the change forced a nervous bark of laughter from him as he waited to see what happened next.

On the screen a single word appeared, written in large text and entirely in English.

"Goodbye? Oh hell. Everybody out of here now! Right now!" Seth yelled at the remaining agents, a half dozen of whom were still performing tasks at various points around the cavern.

They all looked startled for a moment, but one look at his bloodless face was enough to send them running towards the ladder at the exit.

A countdown began on screen, giving them one minute to clear what he could only assume would be a blast radius. Seth dropped the laptop and shoved Lindel ahead of him towards the exit.

"You're sure all the nuclear material is gone?" he shouted at her as they ran.

"The rods were removed hours ago, but I have no idea what was being powered before that!"

"Wait!" Seth yelled as he ground to a halt, "Could that chamber you were examining be some kind of capacitor?"

"I don't know..." Lindel replied in sudden alarm.

"Go," Seth told her. "Clear the surface, there's no telling how big this blast could be."

Without another word he ran back towards the array and his discarded laptop.

"What are you doing?!" Lindel screamed. "You don't even know the language, let alone the programming to disarm it!"

"Maybe not, but before this thing goes nuclear, I owe it to everyone in a thirty-kilometre radius to try. Get to the surface," he told her again, looking her in the eye for one interminable second, before turning his attention back to the laptop.

Lindel stood there for an instant longer, plagued by indecision. If the device went nuclear, no warning at this point would help, but if not, the others on the surface still needed to be warned.

"Good luck," she said simply, before bolting for the ladder.

"See you soon," he replied without looking up.

By the time she'd scrambled to the top of the ladder, Lindel was frantic. At least half the time must have elapsed.

"Run!" She screamed to anyone who might still be nearby even as she followed her own advice.

8:17

"Clear the area! Get as far away as you can!" She shouted again as she exited the house they had hidden the machine under.

The soldier who had blocked her way when she'd first entered the cavern was waiting for her. Lindel didn't even stop as she screamed at him again to run.

"Where's Dr. Gable?!" he asked as he matched her stride for stride.

"I'll explain in a minute, just run, and tell your men to do the same, we've got about fifteen seconds till that thing blows!"

To his credit the man didn't hesitate but pressed the call button on his radio as he kept pace with her.

"All personnel, evacuate the site immediately, take nothing, go now! You've got ten seconds to get to a safe distance!" he said without preamble.

Lindel just kept running, her legs churning in pure terror as the man deliberately moved into line behind her. She was abruptly blasted through the air at the same time the ground cracked and fell away beneath her.

With a sickening thud she came back to earth a few metres beyond the ruined ground and felt her leg snap as she tumbled out of control.

The pain hit her like a hammer as she thudded to a

stop. She couldn't help but let out a terrified scream as she noticed bright white bone sticking through her shin. It was nothing compared to the horror she felt a moment later though as she saw what had happened behind her.

Of the house, nothing was left, even the cavern was gone, replaced by a hundred-metre-wide depression in the land where they had been. All around her there was screaming, and she realised that while she had more or less avoided the flying rubble caused by the explosion, others had been far less lucky.

Seth was dead. She couldn't find it in her heart to even doubt that. Right now though, there were other matters that demanded her attention before she could even allow that thought to sink in.

"Geiger counter!" she yelled at anyone still capable of hearing and obeying. "Someone bring me a Geiger counter. Now!" A few feet away, the soldier who had shielded her with his own body lay. What looked to be a piece of roof tile had impaled him through the neck. As she watched in helpless dismay, he took a last gurgling breath and was still. She tried to crawl to him, but her leg was bent at an impossible angle and the agony of moving it soon made her subside. With a wound like that, CPR wouldn't have helped anyway, some distant part of her mind rationalised.

8:17

"Where's my blasted Geiger counter!" She yelled, her last reserves of adrenaline fading.

A moment later a shadow fell across her and the sound of sirens became audible in the distance.

"Here it is, ma'am," A young soldier with a deep gash across his left cheek and a bloated black eye said as he stumbled to a stop beside her.

Even the machine had taken damage she noted, though it appeared superficial. She flicked it on without taking it from the soldier's possession and pointed the port towards the crater. It began to click, but only as much as the usual slow rate of background radiation implied.

"Not nuclear..." She sighed with a sudden giddy grin, then allowed herself to collapse where she was. She regretted it instantly as her broken leg was once again jostled, demanding her full attention.

"I'll get you an ambulance," the soldier said. "Just try to stay still.

"What about the others?" Lindel asked as she clutched her leg above the break.

"Some are bad, but there's enough of us left mobile to do what needs to be done. Just don't move until the medics arrive."

Lindel could only nod as he hurried away.

She knew she couldn't have saved Seth. She had barely been saved herself, and only because that soldier had placed himself in harm's way to protect her, costing him his life.

Lindel felt suddenly dizzy, and as she laid her head down on the scratchy grass below her, she saw the patch on the man's uniform proclaimed him as Carter.

"Thank you, Carter," she mumbled as she lost consciousness.

CHAPTER 12

"I can't believe it's come to this," Lindel said as she rubbed the full-length cast which covered her left leg from hip to toe. She didn't know which was more stifling, it, or the wheelchair the doctor had confined her to since the abortive mission to Perth nine days gone. As it turned out, the explosion had broken her left leg in four places, not to mention dislocated it at the hip. Thankfully that had been the extent of her injuries apart from a nasty concussion and a few scrapes and bruises. She'd been stuck in hospital until yesterday afternoon, and was more than ready to jump back into the hunt for Seth's killers. Whatever sympathy the awakened may have engendered in either the government or the wider population before Perth had now dissipated in that horrendous blast. An executive order had come down this morning classifying the awakened as enemies of the state. Those already in custody would stay that way, but the declaration paved the way for military intervention in what up until now had been purely a civilian affair.

Normally the thought of their own military targeting private civilians would have disturbed Lindel greatly.

However, although the A.T.U. had superior intelligence gathering capabilities, at least domestically, she was forced to admit they no longer had the weight of firepower this unique situation called for. Several of their teams had suffered critical losses over the last few weeks, and suitable replacements were only now being vetted into service. While she'd been in hospital, the others had been working feverishly to uncover the locations of the remaining ten machines. After a week of frenetic searching, five targets had been located, and a full military strike was about to take place with the A.T.U. acting as a command-and-control hub.

"You know better than anyone why this is necessary," Colonel Chambers remarked in response to her previous statement, though not unkindly. "Are we ready?"

Lindel took a moment to check her displays before nodding. "All stations ready on your order Colonel."

"Very well. All units attain ready position and

report," he ordered without introduction or preamble.

Lindel nodded to her team of communications specialists to pass on the orders, then pressed a button on her console. A bank of screens showing video feeds from each of the five cities sprang to life. The assault commanders all wore cameras, whose feeds were displayed. The biometric readouts from the individual soldiers under their command were shown on a second screen at each station. In a few moments, the operation would begin. It was a joint assault involving both A.T.U. personnel and army units in the cities where their manpower had been reduced below operational levels. They had agreed that Colonel Chambers would oversee the operation in its entirety due to many years of tactical field expertise. Director Illum would act as his primary advisor.

In front of Lindel's desk, the group of comm. specialists sat in a row ready to relay orders to their individual teams.

A few moments later Lindel received the updates and nodded that they had received the confirmations.

"All choppers dust off and execute attack run alpha," Chambers ordered a moment later, and the comm. techs relayed the order.

"Each team is to begin their assault as soon as their bird has finished firing. Captain's discretion," he added, indicating that no further formal attack order would be given.

* * *

It was only moments later that the first chopper appeared, though it felt much longer to Jacinta as she watched the process unfold. For today's operation, she'd been relegated to little more than an observer as the colonel and director took point.

It was the team on the northern outskirts of Melbourne whose feed first showed the chopper come coasting in low above the neighbouring houses. It banked suddenly to fire a barrage of gas canisters through the windows of an abandoned mechanic's building. A man stumbled out, weapon in hand, and a sniper on a nearby roof picked him off before he could fire.

The chopper circled and fired through windows on the rear side of the building, then took off to circle and monitor from a safe distance.

On the other monitors, three more of the choppers had arrived and were performing similar manoeuvres, however the fifth had yet to arrive.

8:17

"Get me a report on chopper five," Chambers barked a moment later when it still didn't appear. The on-ground team was left shuffling their feet as they waited for the air support to materialise, giving the enemy at one of the other safe houses ample opportunity to send them warning.

A moment later the tech in communication with the team in Adelaide turned to face them. "Sir, chopper five is not responding and Commander McClaren has just reported an explosion near his position."

"Bring up the satellite feed for that location," Director Illum ordered Lindel without preamble.

"Tell McClaren to hold for orders," Chambers barked at the tech.

In seconds, the main screen, which sat above all the other stations, had switched to a satellite view of the explosion. A quick zoom showed a plume of black smoke rising from the wreckage of what had to be their chopper.

"Survivors?" Chambers demanded.

"Unknown," Lindel replied. "Movement around the crash site is too obscured to make a determination."

"Blast," Chambers growled even as Director Illum ordered the footage back-traced to see what had gone wrong.

Lindel worked for a moment, causing the screen to flicker and the crash site to disappear, though the location remained unchanged. A moment later they saw the chopper fly in from the south-east. As it neared the inevitable end of its flight, a bar of bright green light appeared from somewhere off screen. It only lasted a second, but it was long enough to cause the helicopter to explode violently and fall unchecked from the sky.

"Track the origin of that weapon," Director Illum ordered.

"And get another bird in the air," Chambers added. "I want it prepped for a full missile strike as soon as whatever defences they've set up have been cleared."

"That was no handheld pistol," Jacinta commented as Lindel rewound the footage again and expanded the view. They tracked the origin of the blast to a block south of where McClaren's team was stationed. It appeared to have originated in the attic of a non-descript house.

"Give me infrared on that site," Illum ordered.

"Commander McClaren requesting orders," the tech assigned to his team announced.

"Continue holding, new directives to follow," Chambers returned as he studied the monitors showing the progress of the other teams' assaults.

8:17

The attacks in Melbourne and Alice Springs were progressing well, though casualties were mounting. The fight in Cairns was all but over, the team there having fared particularly well for some reason which could be assessed at a later date. In Brisbane, the attack was now bogged down in a fire fight, an unacceptable outcome due to the enemy's superior weaponry,

"Alert the team at site three they have incoming, and tell chopper three I want a long-range missile strike on that property. Everything they're carrying," Chambers called to the appropriate tech.

"That's it then," Lindel said, drawing both Director Illum, and Chambers' attention back to her station. The main screen now showed an infrared image of the wider area. Three distinct buildings had been marked at locations in a rough triangle surrounding the property McClaren's team was supposed to be raiding right now.

"Talk to me," Chambers ordered.

"Infrared scans show this installation guarded by two hostiles at the blast's origin point. It appears to be some form of advanced weapon system. Subsequent imaging of the area reveals two more similar sites here and here," Lindel responded with brevity.

"Good work, get those locations to McClaren's team. Put me on with McClaren," he ordered the appropriate tech a moment later.

"Ready sir," an anxious voice called back over the comm link.

"Commander, new intel is coming to your team as we speak. Your bird is down. Some form of advanced, yet stationary anti-aircraft weapon system took it out. I need you to abort your current mission and pull back to a safe distance from the target. Using the data I'm sending you, split your team into four squads. Team one, two and three will each move on one of the identified targets, which appear to be manned by only a pair of guards apiece. Use of snipers is advised and approved if viable. Team four is to move into position near our downed bird and secure any survivors and the crash site as soon as that emplacement is taken out."

"Got it. Data received, beginning withdrawal," McClaren responded.

"Cairns team reports no further resistance, position secured." One of the tech's announced.

"Might I suggest ordering them to withdraw to a distance of three hundred metres and cordoning off the area," Lindel interjected.

Chambers looked at her leg cast for an instant before nodding.

"Relay that," Chambers ordered the tech, whilst briefly placing a comforting hand on Lindel's shoulder.

A sudden flare on one of the screens drew everyone's attention, but it was only the chopper at the Brisbane site following Chambers' orders. When the explosion cleared, the satellite imagery showed a coordinated assault of the property beginning in earnest, and Chambers nodded to himself before moving on.

The attack in Alice Springs had swung their way, however the Melbourne site had become a bloody affair. A full half of their force had been confirmed killed or injured, and the remaining hostiles had withdrawn to their underground cavern. Their retreat had given his forces a chance to regroup and evacuate the wounded, but storming that cavern would not go well. Chambers began running various scenarios through his head as to how to get them out without sustaining massive casualties, or risk detonating the main weapon with explosives or gunfire.

"Commander McClaren reports his teams are in position," the tech called a few moments later.

"Proceed," Chambers ordered, then turned to face the infrared image from the satellite feed.

At the target to the northeast, sniper fire felled the two hostiles inside without a pause, and the squad there took the position unhindered. To the west, the sniper fire proved partially effective, taking down one hostile and wounding another. The remainder of the squad breached the room, but instead of firing back, the hostile shot at the weapon platform, causing it to violently explode. The sudden flash blinded the satellite for a moment. When the feed returned to normal, the building which was housing it, along with both their squad and the hostile, was gone.

"Son of a… warn McClaren not to hit those weapon platforms!" Chambers yelled, the tech responsible scrambling to obey.

The third site, where the blast had felled their chopper to the south had no reliable sniper points nearby. McClaren's team was about to breach the room in a frontal assault when the new order went through. It alerted the two hostiles inside to their presence somehow though, and they abruptly began firing their weapons right through the wall at McClaren's men forcing them to dive for cover. One of the soldiers threw a flashbang through one of the resulting holes and his two companions nearer the door hauled themselves up and bounded into the room. The stun grenade had done its job well, and moments later the two targets were disarmed and captive, the weapon emplacement intact.

"Order delta squad to move in on the chopper site, then put me through to McClaren," Chambers said in a no-nonsense tone. Somehow his team had avoided any casualties despite the ambush, and the tech reported McClaren was on the line a moment later.

"What's going on, Sir, we felt an explosion?" McClaren asked breathlessly.

"Alpha squad subdued their hostiles with sniper fire, no casualties. I'm sorry Commander, but a hostile at bravo site used his weapon to fire at the target and took the entire building with him, apart from the sniper they positioned prior to entry, we're not reading any survivors."

"Commander Gentry reports the Alice Springs site is secure," One of the techs called out.

That's two, Chambers thought, *maybe three with the assault in Melbourne remaining at a standstill.*

"Brisbane site also now reporting secure," Another tech announced unexpectedly.

"E.T.A. on the replacement bird?" Chambers asked.

"Two minutes thirty," the tech called back after consulting with someone on the other end of a line.

"Lindel, how deep are those caverns," Director Illum asked.

"The two I've seen were consistent at approximately thirty metres," She replied thoughtfully.

"But that was to the floor, yes? How far from ground level to the roof of the cavern?"

Chambers started smiling while Lindel thought for a moment.

"No more than three to five metres I would imagine," she replied, understanding dawning as she said it.

"Order Commander Orson to place heavy demolition charges around the perimeter of the target building and collapse that cavern," Chambers ordered without remorse. "And remind him to detonate from a distance of at least three hundred metres."

The tech relayed the orders and a tense wait ensued while Orsen's men placed the heavy charges, which they first had to retrieve from their vehicles.

"Commander McClaren reports crash site secure and first responders onsite, no survivors."

Chambers felt his lips thin slightly at the news,

expected though it was. "Order McClaren's team to regroup and assemble at their original go point. If the missile strike is a success, we'll continue the operation. Lindel, find out how many hostiles the other teams encountered, I need some idea if we even still have sufficient manpower to accomplish the mission."

Lindel nodded and began issuing instructions to the three techs whose teams had completed their assignments.

"Commander Orson reporting ready Colonel, but is requesting confirmation that the falling debris won't detonate the machine."

Chambers clenched his fists as he thought about what to tell the Melbourne assault team leader. The truth was he had no idea if the machine could even be set off that way. They were clearly volatile under the right circumstances. The one in Perth had exploded when Doctor Gable had accessed its programming and met a preconditioned response. The anti-air weapon Chambers' men had been killed by had been hit by an energy-based weapon fired by someone who presumably knew its design specs and weak spots. Both intentional outcomes. On the other hand, if the Melbourne cavern was anything like the others, he could order a hundred men down that ladder and the entrenched enemy could pick them off at their leisure. They would have plenty of time to detonate the weapon or come up with some other nasty surprise, either result would lead to a failed mission. No, if he was going to do this, it had to be now.

Taking a deep breath Chambers asked for a direct link to Orson.

"Commander, I'm sorry to say I can't give you that guarantee; however we have no other viable options to proceed. Under no circumstances can we allow these people to remain in control of a nuclear-powered weapon, whatever the cost. Make sure everyone is behind the three-hundred-metre line and proceed as ordered."

There was a moment of hesitation over the line and then a hesitant response.

"Acknowledged."

It was a remarkably stoic reply from a man about to take an action that might or might not set off a nuclear blast of indeterminate size.

"Commander McClaren reporting in, Colonel," Lindel announced. "Remaining members of his team are either ready to breach or in over watch. The chopper is on station and awaiting go orders. Other team leaders are reporting between ten and fourteen hostiles at captured sites."

8:17

Chambers did a quick assessment in his head as he thought about the six hostiles already neutralised, then factored in the losses McClaren's team had endured. The enemy would have been alerted to their presence by the attack on the anti-air positions. However, the heavy payload the chopper was carrying should significantly reduce the threat level the surviving hostiles could bring to bear. He decided that despite the fluid situation, the losses on either side should more or less cancel each other out. The overwhelming force of the coming attack would hopefully counter any loss of surprise on their part. "Tell McClaren the threat matrix remains steady. He is a go once the bird has expended its missiles. Then order the bird to begin its run."

"Yes Colonel," Lindel replied.

The feed monitoring the Melbourne site shuddered for a long moment before coming to rest at a slight angle as the charges Orson's men had set went off. The ground around the site held a moment longer, then fell away in a great crash and roar. Everyone in the room held their breath, though their fear would be nothing compared to that of the men on the ground. A few seconds later the bedrock came to rest at the bottom of the cavern, but there was no further explosion. The apex of the device could be seen breaching the top of the rubble, largely undamaged from what little they could see.

Eventually, someone audibly expelled a breath.

"I want confirmation that site is secure," Chambers said quietly a moment later as dust continued to rise from the crater.

That just left Adelaide, where the replacement attack chopper was just now beginning its run.

The screen showed several missile trails launched from a distance, then a flash off screen as the weapons hit their target. The chopper fired again, and then the camera, mounted on McClaren's helmet began a quick sprint towards the now demolished house. A body lay in the yard. Well, some of it anyway, as McClaren's team moved in without resistance.

Fortunately the tunnel to the underground cavern had been cleared by the explosion, and McClaren dropped a flash bang down the hole without even checking it first. The instant it detonated he climbed onto the first rung and used the sidebars to slide the rest of the way down. Pulling his gun up as he hit the ground, he entered the cavern and began stalking the room whilst his team filed down behind him.

"Where are they all?" Jacinta asked, shattering the tensely quiet atmosphere of the control room.

8:17

A line of green light split the screen and gunfire followed. McClaren's camera turned to the source of the blast as a body crumpled and another line of light came from his other side. This time the response was too slow though, and just as McClaren turned his head, a man holding one of the awakened's advanced pistols disappeared back into the wall.

McClaren was not inexperienced though, and ordered his team to form a circle and guard the walls.

A moment later the man appeared again a quarter way around the cavern. He stayed just long enough to fire off a shot and then melt back into the wall for a third time. Again a few seconds passed, and the man ducked out from behind the enormous machine that dominated the room. His aim was excellent and two of the soldiers fell screaming, one on either side of the circle. Once again the man disappeared into the wall, return gunfire ricocheting ineffectively off the stone.

More seconds passed as the soldiers scanned the room, ready to fire the instant they had a target.

"Where is he?" Chambers muttered a moment later when the hostile still had not appeared.

"Where could he do the most damage?" Director Illum mused.

"Oh hell," Jacinta muttered as she dived for the

comm. station and shouted into the mic., "McClaren, behind you!"

The man reacted fast; she'd give him that. As he spun, his camera feed showed an arm already clear of the ground within the circle of still standing soldiers. Before the hostile could fully emerge, McClaren dived towards him and ripped the small device strapped to his wrist away from his body. Something he touched made the device power down, and after a momentary spasm the limb went limp. The rest of its owner now becoming permanently relegated to the confines of the cavern's bedrock.

"Commander Orson reports Melbourne site secure, Colonel," Lindel relayed into the gap.

Chambers nodded and continued to wait while McClaren ordered the majority of his men to fan out and secure the room whilst the others tended the wounded. It was clear the men in that cavern were on edge, but the area was small, and they efficiently executed their orders, no doubt keenly aware their comrades couldn't be evacuated until the room was secured.

After the search was complete, McClaren ordered his men back into a defensive formation. When another few moments had passed and no further challenge was forthcoming, he declared the site secure. He wasn't taking any chances though as he ordered his men to remain in formation while the injured were evacuated.

"Adelaide site reporting secured," Lindel added a moment later. "All sites secured."

Chambers nodded in satisfaction as a round of congratulations swept through the team.

"How many did we lose?" Chambers asked bluntly.

The few short words silenced the room.

Lindel consulted with her techs for a moment as they revised the numbers from the bio readouts on each soldier's suit.

She turned back to the colonel a moment later with a grim expression.

"Counting all sites and the downed bird we had sixty-one KIA and twenty-three wounded, Colonel."

"My God," Director Illum breathed in shock. "That's nearly half of the total forces we committed to this operation."

"The butcher took his pound of flesh today," Chambers agreed.

"Find me the rest of these people Jeff. I want them gone, and their machines with them," Chambers remarked before leaving the room without further comment. Jacinta couldn't help but notice as he walked away that his left hand was clenched so tight the blood had flowed away, leaving it white and sallow.

Human after all, Jacinta thought briefly.

"Lindel, have any prisoners rounded up and transported back to A.T.U. headquarters for immediate interrogation, then join us on the floor," Director Illum ordered.

"Jacinta, with me. We have work to do."

CHAPTER 13

"I think I have enough to take a run at Sarah," Jacinta told Jeff as she approached his desk.

"Is that really necessary?" the director replied, we'll soon have other prisoners of a more appropriate age for interrogation.

"I've been recording my sessions with Victoria," Jacinta continued without acknowledging Jeff's statement. "Looking for any tells or honest information I've been able to get from her."

"I know. How do the two relate?"

"Do you remember what I told you about the way the patients were acting right before we released them from Saint Patrick's?" She asked in return.

The director nodded, obviously remembering what had at the time seemed a wild story about the patients behaving in an oddly coordinated fashion.

"You still think that little girl is somehow in charge of their entire operation?"

"I know how it sounds," Jacinta replied. "Under normal circumstances I wouldn't even consider the possibility..."

"These are far from normal circumstances though…" Jeff interjected. "So why wait this long if you really believe she's the one?"

Jacinta thought for a moment.

"If I'm right, she's been fooling us all since day one. She's calm, in control, has no visible tells, and the face of an innocent. If she really is in charge, and can still operate with that level of composure, I need something major that will crack her in one fell swoop. Chipping away at that type of personality would only make her more determined to resist."

"And you think your sessions with Victoria have provided you with an angle that will work?" Jeff asked.

Jacinta nodded. "I think so, yes. I might end up just making a fool of myself, but in all honesty, if this doesn't work I've run out of other ideas."

"All right," he said after a moment. "I'll allow it. What's your play?"

Jacinta raised her eyebrow. "You may as well come and see for yourself. I'll need a witness in the room while interrogating a minor, anyway."

"Okay, this should prove interesting."

8:17

*   *   *

A few minutes later Jacinta opened the door to Sarah's cell and preceded Jeff into the room. The space had been modified into something of a bedroom for the sake of their smallest prisoner, and Jacinta moved to sit at the table across from the young girl, who was idly sketching dots onto a piece of paper.

"Agent Robbins, it's been some time," the little girl greeted her as Jeff moved unobtrusively into a corner.

"Give it up Sarah," Jacinta said forcefully. "Victoria has betrayed you. We know who you are, what you're doing here, and how to stop you."

The little girl looked up from her drawing and studied Jacinta for a long moment before returning to the sketch.

"I doubt that," she remarked without looking back.

Jacinta looked over to the two-sided mirror and clicked her fingers in a prearranged signal to the technician in the next room. A monitor in the corner came to life, showing the bare cell Victoria was confined within. At one side of the table Victoria's recorded image sat, on the other side, Jacinta's back.

She'd arranged the interviews that way purposefully so that the footage could be altered later. She'd had the techs dub another track of her voice over the visuals to warp the meaning of Victoria's answers. This was her last real chance to break through the girl's wall of silence, but this conversation would still have to be steered very carefully. If it got even a little off track, the altered footage would be out of order, and worse than useless.

"What do you want this time?" pre-recorded Victoria asked bluntly.

"I want to know why you're doing this. Why the conspiracy? Who or what is your target?"

"You," Victoria spoke calmly. "People. Humans."

"Don't be ridiculous," Jacinta's dubbed voice replied. "You're every bit as human as I am. Theatrics aside, we have your date and place of birth, your social security number, and any number of data points which show you've led a rich full life. At least until you were assaulted and left for dead. You spent months as a Jane Doe in a coma, and then, this..."

"Really?" Victoria replied in mock earnestness, "Please, do tell."

"That nonsense about your location being on the moon... did you really expect us to think you were from outer space?"

Victoria shrugged. "It amused me to think that you might," she admitted. "But in the end it was never meant to be more than a simple bit of theatre that kept you chasing your own tails while my people worked."

She motioned the tech in the next room to pause the feed.

"Pay special attention here Sarah, this is where it gets interesting."

She motioned again, and the feed resumed.

"But why the machines, and why underground? If your people aren't after money or power, what do you want?"

"All right, I'll throw you a bone," the image eventually replied. "It doesn't matter what you think of what we're doing, or what orders you have from your superiors. I promise you that the more of our machines you take offline around the world, the worse it will be for you when the time comes to fulfil their task."

"So this is a global effort. You're all in this together?" Jacinta's dubbed voice said in mock surprise.

"Yes. It goes without saying that the more of them that are online the better our chances will be. We'll need them soon."

"So let me see if I understand this. In your mind, by stealing forty-eight nuclear fuel rods and using them to power a global array of energy-based weapons you're what... protecting us?"

"Of course," dubbed Victoria replied, giving a seemingly straight answer to a question which had never been asked.

Jacinta motioned again, and the feed went blank.

She moved around to the side of the table and sat on the small chair opposite the young girl.

"I know you're in charge Sarah. I remember how Victoria reacted to you that first day in the hospital. She was goading me, but a single word from you silenced her and changed her behaviour entirely."

For the first time Sarah looked up, and that same disturbingly adult expression which had set Jacinta so on edge back at the hospital had finally returned.

"It was a nice try," she said. "But it's edited."

"What do you mean?" Jacinta frowned.

"You got some of the basic details wrong. And Victoria isn't a good enough liar to say those things with a straight face in the context you presented."

Jacinta sat back in her chair with a satisfied smile as Jeff stopped leaning against the wall and came over to join them.

"Which part was wrong? The part about the machines, or the part about you helping us?"

"How can I help you?" Sarah replied, the childish persona resumed in full force. "I'm only seven, and mum says I'm cute, but short."

She looked Jeff in the eye before giving him an unpleasant smile.

"This is all some kind of game to you, isn't it?" Jeff prodded as Sarah went back to drawing.

"I assure you Director Illum, this is the most serious thing I will ever do in my life."

"If it's that important, tell us about it. Maybe if we understand what you're doing, we might find some common ground."

Sarah continued drawing her dots, the paper almost full. There was no other response.

When it became clear the conversation would go no further, Jeff inclined his head and Jacinta followed suit as he stood and headed towards the door.

"You'll be wanting this," Sarah called as she turned to leave.

"What is it?" Jacinta asked as she took possession of the drawing Sarah had been working on since before their arrival.

Sarah shrugged. "Call it what you will. An omen, a harbinger, a portent to the apocalypse. Suffice it to say, if you come to an understanding of what it means before *my* people finish their work, your fate is already sealed."

* * *

"What do you think it is?" Jeff asked once they'd left the room. He was still studying the page full of dots, which looked for all the world to Jacinta like the seven-year-old's scribble it might actually be.

"Who knows? Another code maybe, or just another game like Victoria's fake location coordinates. These people have a knack for getting under our skin, but I'll give it to Lindel just in case."

There was a commotion further down the corridor and Jameson's authoritative voice could be heard dressing down a subordinate.

"You just let them take her?"

"They had all the proper documentation, Sir," a voice replied.

Jacinta glanced at Jeff, whose forehead was now furrowed in a frown as he picked up the pace. The two of them rounded a corner to find Jameson red-faced and livid as he noticed their approach.

"You're dismissed," Jameson said tersely before turning towards them.

"Director, Ma'am," he said, causing her lips to thin slightly in irritation. "It seems Colonel Chambers has taken Victoria off site to a military facility with full authorization from the Prime Minister."

"What!" Jacinta barked. "We need her here. Jeff, except for maybe Sarah, I'm convinced Victoria knows more about what the awakened are doing than any other prisoner we have. Her continued interrogation is the best chance we have of stopping whatever they're planning."

Jameson handed a thin folder over to Director Illum, who perused the contents.

"These are real. I'll get in touch with Canberra, but for now there's nothing more we can do."

"I don't understand," Jacinta replied. "Even if this is a legitimate transfer, why do the military suddenly want her so badly?"

Jeff just shook his head.

"I don't know, but I don't like it. This smacks of an urgency our current information has no basis for. I'll get back to you once I know more."

CHAPTER 14

Three days had passed since Jeff made that promise, and so far the silence from the political higher-ups had been deafening.

Jacinta opened the small wall safe in her linen cupboard and withdrew her gun and I.D.

With the ease of long practice she clicked the ammo cartridge into place and holstered the weapon after glancing to make sure the safety was on. She closed the safe and linen cupboard before heading out, grabbing the keys from their place near the door.

She headed out the interconnecting door to the garage and unlocked the sixty-seven mustang convertible she'd owned since she was twenty-three. It had taken her years of after-school jobs and whatever other money she could scrounge up to save up for one. But then she'd always been focused on the long game, even as a child. Jacinta got in and turned the key, feeling the two hundred and eighty-nine cubic inch V8 engine growl to life without complaint. She pressed the button on her keyring that opened the garage door and waited for it to cycle open.

The door was less than halfway up when two army Humvee's came speeding into view. At the last second they changed course and mounted the curb to halt with a screech of tyres directly in front of her driveway.

The instant they stopped, half a dozen soldiers poured out of the vehicles and pointed weapons at her. A sergeant stepped out a moment later.

"Agent Robbins," the young man called. "Please step out of the vehicle, I have orders to take you into custody."

Jacinta opened the car door. With the pair of Humvee's blocking her exit from the garage, the vehicle was useless to her even if she'd wanted to escape.

She turned off the engine and slowly got out of the car, careful not to make any overt moves with half a dozen rifles pointed her way.

"I'm a private citizen, not military. You don't have the authority to arrest me. What is this all about?"

"No idea Ms. Robbins, but my orders are clear, bring you to Rush Base for debriefing, without delay."

Jacinta raised an eyebrow. Without delay likely meant that if she didn't cooperate, they would force her into one of the Humvees and take her anyway.

Deciding the odds were not in her favour, she nodded to the sergeant.

"Very well, whose orders?" she asked as she left the confines of the garage.

"General Blake, ma'am."

"Gun," one of the soldiers called sharply.

She gave the pimply soldier a withering stare.

"I'm a high-ranking member of the A.T.U. Of course I have a sidearm."

The sergeant held out a hand without a word, and Jacinta sighed before slowly walking forward and handing over the weapon.

"And your phone please."

"I'd better get those back," she said as she placed the items in his hand.

"Yes ma'am. We should go."

Jacinta fished in her pocket for a moment before finding the button that would close the garage door, then followed the sergeant into the back seat of the nearest vehicle. Seeing her cooperating, the other soldiers piled back into the Humvee's at the sergeant's order. The moment they were seated, the doors were closed, and the drivers had them racing along suburban streets in what was no doubt an interesting, if not entirely alarming sight for the residents.

"You know, when I don't turn up to the A.T.U. on time they're going to send people looking for me."

"Now that we have you secured, Agent Robbins, Director Illum is being advised to that effect."

"I see, so this *is* an officially sanctioned action then?"

"Yes ma'am. That's all I know. The General will explain once we reach the base."

Jacinta sat back in the seat, trying not to appear as worried as she was. What could a top-level army General want with her? The A.T.U. was an intelligence division of the civilian government. It wasn't part of the military structure at all, making this little more than a sanctioned kidnapping.

The two vehicles sped through the streets, heading north as they made their way to Rush Base. They pulled up at the front gate and the sergeant had them admitted past the checkpoint in moments.

They must have been expecting us, Jacinta thought warily.

The small convoy zoomed through the base's streets until they came to a low-set concrete building whose purpose was obscured by any lack of specific architectural detail. The Humvees stopped at the front door and the sergeant exited the vehicle, motioning for her to do the same. As soon as she was out, one of the soldiers closed the door behind her and the vehicles drove away.

"This way please," the sergeant said, heading for the front door.

Jacinta looked around, but this far into the base there was little point trying to make a run for it.

The sergeant stopped to see why she wasn't following, and she took a step before he could turn and see her hesitation. Once she'd caught up, he began walking again, even opening the door for her when they arrived.

They passed another checkpoint just as easily as the first, though this one was manned by an MP. Then she was led down a long corridor filled with cells on one side, and sealed rooms on the other.

"Where are you taking me?" Jacinta asked again.

The sergeant didn't answer for a long moment, but then stopped in front of a door with the letters IR-6 stencilled above the frame.

8:17

"The General will be with you shortly, please wait in here."

"An interrogation room?" Jacinta asked, her pulse racing. What could she have done that warranted this extreme treatment?

"Yes, but not for you. Please step inside Agent Robbins."

Jacinta just looked at him for a long moment as he pulled a keycard from his pocket and unlocked the door, opening it and motioning her inside.

She looked into the room, expecting to see a solid table and a few chairs. Instead, it was the other side of a cell, the one where she could watch the subject through the large pane of one-way glass. A technician was manning a desk not dissimilar from the one at the A.T.U. and the room was dimmed so that whoever occupied the cell couldn't see in.

The sergeant nodded at her again, and Jacinta stepped inside, causing the technician to look up momentarily before going back to his work. The sergeant closed the door behind her, and Jacinta moved into the middle of the room. Beyond the glass was an empty table with metal loops through which handcuffs could be fastened, just like the one she'd feared was in store for her. A chair sat on either side of the table, but aside from that the cell was empty.

She couldn't help but pace the cramped confines of the monitoring room.

"I don't suppose you can tell me what's going on?" she said without much hope.

"Sorry Ma'am. The General will brief you when he arrives."

Jacinta rolled her eyes.

"Any idea when that will..."

She was interrupted by the door opening again, through which a large man, who appeared to be in his late fifties, strode. His manner was as controlled and pressed as the perfectly fitting uniform he wore. A uniform whose name tag pronounce him Aiden Blake.

"Thank you for coming, Agent Robbins," he said without preamble.

Jacinta raised an eyebrow at the choice of phrasing, but let him continue.

"As you know, we took Victoria Jones into custody three days ago after the A.T.U. failed to extract the necessary information from her or any of the other awakened."

"Have you had a different result?" Jacinta asked.

"Not at first, but an hour ago she finally cracked, agreeing to tell us everything."

8:17

"What did she say?" Jacinta demanded. All the potential answers she'd been looking for since the day of the awakening spinning through her mind.

"Nothing. She clammed up once she'd told us she was willing to talk. Claimed she would only reveal her information to you."

"So that's what this is all about?" Jacinta fumed. "You didn't have to abduct me out of my driveway, a simple phone call to the A.T.U. would have done the trick."

"I apologise for that, but time is of the essence. We're not sure why she chose now to break. Her interrogator wasn't even in the room when she began demanding to speak to me. All I know is that she is growing ever more anxious."

The door on the other side of the glass opened, and a soldier escorted a defiant Victoria to the seat opposite them. He secured her handcuffs to the loop on the table, then left again without a word.

"Time to see what all this is about," Blake said in a tone a half-hair short of a command.

Jacinta looked across at Victoria. The dark-skinned woman was staring right at them as if she could see through the one-way mirror.

Jacinta nodded.

"Well past time," she agreed, passing the General and heading for the corridor. She entered the brightly lit hallway, walked a dozen steps to the next door, and took a deep breath.

She turned the handle.

CHAPTER 15

Jacinta opened the door and strode into the room with as much confidence as she could bring to bear. She was an experienced interrogator, but Victoria had stymied her again and again over the last few months.

It was beyond frustrating.

"I heard you had something to tell me?" She said as she took the seat opposite the British woman.

"It's not what I wanted," Victoria returned with a frown, her usual unreadable demeanour gone, replaced now with something akin to concern. "However, events are proceeding more quickly than intended, and we have run out of time."

"I see." Jacinta leaned back in her chair and waited for Victoria to continue. From experience, she knew that anything she said might set the mercurial woman off, so she waited.

Victoria's frown deepened when she realised Jacinta had said all she intended to.

"You need to let us finish our work. If you had any brains at all, you would aid us."

"Aid you?" Jacinta blurted.

That was new.

"What could possibly inspire us to aid the work of nuclear terrorists?"

"Oh, I don't know. Your survival perhaps?"

"Yes, I've heard these threats before. They're not convincing."

Victoria's hands clenched and unclenched in what Jacinta could only interpret as deep frustration. It didn't fit.

"Look, Victoria, I can see you think you're trying to help us by telling me this, but you're also leaving out some pretty critical information. How can I even begin to trust you when you won't tell me who your intended target is?"

Victoria looked away for a second, her eyes unfocusing as though conversing with someone over a phone call only she could hear.

Jacinta frowned and glanced back through the one-way mirror, knowing that the tech would be scanning the woman with every method they had. Victoria seemed to return to herself and pursed her lips.

8:17

"I'm not allowed to tell you. There is still a seven-point-nine percent chance our plan will proceed as intended. Your people are tenacious, I'll grant you that. We expected far less resistance. We expected to have six times as many weapons completed by now, and due to the vast amounts of ocean on this planet, their coverage would always have been spotty. At any rate, we've done what we can while you run around sowing the seeds of your own destruction."

"If you're doing all this for the good of humanity, why wouldn't you simply tell our leaders what needs to be done and why. If there is a clear and present threat to our survival, we're not going to ignore it."

"You would have, having no way to confirm it by yourselves. Even now that is beyond you, and by the time you realised your mistake, there would have been no time for you to do anything about it. In a little under nine hours we will know if our strike will be effective. If it is, the completed weapons will implode, and you will never hear from us again."

Jacinta felt the hair on the back of her neck stand upright. They had a timetable.

Wait. That was the good option?

"And if not?" she prompted when Victoria lapsed into silence.

"Then your species stands on the brink of extinction."

Jacinta just shook her head. In the last few days since the army had sequestered Victoria, she'd forgotten how manipulative she could be.

"We've been over this repeatedly, Victoria. You and I are the same species. We have records, photos, and firsthand witnesses to your childhood in England. You didn't appear magically after the awakening, and talking about yourself in this manner isn't going to convince us to do anything, except question your sanity."

Victoria laughed, and it was almost manic.

"Fine. When your world is attacked by…"

Her head slammed down on the table, and Jacinta was sure that if her cuffs hadn't been secured to the loops Victoria would have simply slid from her chair.

Jacinta jumped up, looking wildly around the room for some form of attack, before realising that whatever had felled the dark-skinned woman had been internal, and not from an outside assault.

She moved to the other side of the table and felt for a pulse, which was steady and strong. Wondering if the woman had been brought down by a stroke. She secured Victoria's head as a pair of medics rushed in, accompanied by the same guard who had escorted Victoria into the cell.

The woman was unconscious, her nose bleeding profusely from its impact with the table. One of the medics shone a torch in her eyes, checking for a response before frowning.

"We need to move her."

The guard unlocked the cuffs from the table loop and reattached them to a gurney which yet another medic was wheeling in. The first two placed her on it, and headed off to the infirmary as Jacinta was left standing by the table, wondering what had just happened. It took a moment, but General Blake joined her from where he'd been monitoring their conversation.

"What was that?" he demanded. "Has this kind of thing happened before?"

"No," Jacinta muttered. "This is new."

"You were just starting to get somewhere too," Blake said in frustration.

Jacinta nodded, her brow furrowed in deep thought.

"That's just it. We *were* getting somewhere. Then halfway through what seemed like she was actually giving us what she believed to be an honest answer… This."

"The timing is quite unfortunate, but what are you suggesting? To me it appeared as if she had some kind of medical issue, a stroke maybe, or an aneurism."

"I agree. But did you notice her staring off blankly for a moment, earlier in the conversation, as if she was listening to someone we couldn't hear?"

"I did, but we checked for signals when it happened and there was nothing. Given what just occurred, I would have to guess that it was a precursor to whatever caused her to lose consciousness."

Jacinta nodded slowly. It all made sense, but only in the context of here and now. None of the awakened's advanced technology could be explained by Victoria having some kind of brain dysfunction. There had to be more to it than that.

There was a sharp knock on the door, and one of the medics entered.

"Report," General Blake ordered.

"Sir, the prisoner is awake and lucid.

"Good work."

"No Sir," the medic replied. "We hadn't quite reached the infirmary when she woke up on her own."

"What would cause that?"

"Sir, I have no idea. She was comatose and unresponsive, and then she wasn't. I've never seen anything like it. If I didn't know better, I'd swear someone turned her off, and then back on again a few moments later."

Blake scowled. "Take us to her."

"Yes, Sir," the medic responded before turning crisply and leading them down the long corridor, around a corner, through a secured door and into the infirmary.

Only two of the beds were occupied. One with a soldier in traction who had two broken legs, the other with Victoria, secured by her cuffs to the rail of the bed.

She was sitting up, but her shoulders were slumped, and there was a defeated look on her face which hadn't been there before.

"Care to tell us what that was all about?" Jacinta asked as they approached.

"Strangely enough, yes. But I can't. If I say anything more now, I won't be able to help you later. And believe me, you'll want that help."

"So this was all just another game then?"

"Not this time. I understand your frustration Agent

Robbins, but we all have our orders, do we not?"

"Orders? Wait, I thought Victoria was in charge?" Blake demanded with displeasure.

"She coordinated the safe house where we found the first machine. Other awakened protected her, putting her safety above their own lives. If there's someone above her in their hierarchy, the A.T.U. has no knowledge of this individual. The way these people operate though, if there is someone higher up, their leader might not even be in this country. There are awakened all over the world on whom we still have little to no data."

It was true, to a certain point. She had never submitted a formal report on her feeling that the young girl, Sarah, was in charge of this entire operation, as counterintuitive as that seemed. She doubted General Blake would appreciate the distinction, but she couldn't risk Sarah being whisked away by the military the same way Victoria had been.

"Lovely."

"Is there anything else you needed from me, General?"

Blake stared daggers at Victoria for a moment, then let out a breath and shook his head.

8:17

"It seems not. Thank you for your input, Agent Robbins. Wait here and I'll have someone take you back home."

She was about to say 'thank you' out of reflex, but the General was already walking away.

CHAPTER 16

Nine hours had passed since Victoria's ominous deadline, and Jacinta was back at A.T.U. headquarters, sitting opposite a table from a furious Director Illum.

Upon learning of her experience earlier that morning, Jeff had placed several harshly worded protests with the powers that be. Since the army had returned her unharmed an hour after the forced escort to their base though, his objections were gaining little traction.

Between them sat the remains of a platter which had held dozens of sushi rolls only an hour past. It was the only one of three with food still remaining, which Jeff had ordered a low-level agent to pick up for the office. They all expected it to be a late night.

"We should get back out there," Director Illum said. "If Victoria was being literal, we should receive word of an event in the next few minutes."

8:17

Jacinta nodded as she chewed the last bite of her teriyaki chicken roll and stood.

"For the first time, I actually hope she's playing with us," Jacinta said once she'd swallowed her food.

"It feels different this time," Jeff commented with a frown.

She nodded curtly in agreement, and they headed back out onto the floor. Jacinta moved to confer with her analyst group while the director monitored the main data collection stations.

"Anything?" she asked as she entered the somewhat secluded area where Lindel, Mike, and Andrea were scanning through updates for any sign of what Victoria had been referring to. Seth's desk was still empty. She'd considered hiring another analyst, but truth be told, his skill set had so far proven impossible to replace.

"Nothing yet," Andrea said as she read.

Long moments passed while Jacinta stood there, heart beating faster than it should.

"I hate that woman," she said after several minutes had uneventfully passed.

The ringing of Lindel's secure phone sent a shiver down Jacinta's spine. She knew she wasn't the only one that felt it either, since the others all stopped and looked at her as if straining to hear the other end of the conversation.

Lindel picked it up, her expression changing from pleasant to curious, then wide eyed panic as she began frantically pulling a data feed up on her monitor.

At first Jacinta didn't understand what she was seeing. The screen turned black with several hundred white dots scattered randomly throughout.

She'd seen that pattern before somewhere.

"What am I looking at?" she asked as Lindel put down the phone.

Lindel held up a finger and pulled up an accompanying file full of some advanced math which Jacinta had no idea how to interpret.

Lindel just read the information again and again before flicking back to the pattern.

She sat back in her chair, shoulders slumped, mouth opening and closing.

"Lindel," Jacinta said, placing a hand on the deeply troubled woman's shoulder.

The analyst just looked at her blankly for a moment.

"That was Dr. Raynolds from NASA. There's about

to be an announcement to every government in the world, but I asked him to let me know if anything further unusual occurred in the vicinity of Victoria's fake comm. signal."

"And…" Jacinta prompted when Lindel once again fell into her own thoughts.

"We've lost sight of Sirius A."

Jacinta raised an eyebrow.

"Sorry. There's only one thing that could cause a star to disappear like that, and that's another body moving between Earth and that star, blocking our line of sight."

"Are we in danger?" Mike asked from the next desk.

"It's too early to say. Initial observations suggest the object will pass just outside the moon, but we'll have a better idea in the coming hours as we turn our higher resolution telescopes on it. Whatever it is, it has to be big to block out a star even if it's already within our solar system."

Jacinta didn't know what to say, and so stared at the screen as if it could give her the answers she so desperately needed.

"I've seen this before," she said under her breath.

"This couldn't be what Victoria was warning you

about? She couldn't possibly have known days ago what our best scientists have only just discovered," Andrea reminded them. "We should keep scanning the feeds."

Jacinta looked over at the pragmatic woman and nodded for her to continue working.

She stood up, icy fingers working their way down her spine. "It wasn't Victoria who warned me. Lindel, pull up the scan of Sarah's drawing."

Lindel looked at her, eyebrows shooting up as she realised Jacinta's meaning. A few seconds later she'd retrieved the appropriate file and placed the image of the seven-year-old girl's scribble next to the star field. They didn't match.

"I was sure…"

Lindel studied the two images for a long moment, then reframed the size of the image she'd received from Dr. Raynolds.

It was closer, but still wrong. There were far too many dots on the drawing, though she hadn't noticed until now that a small section near the middle of the page had been left blank. Was that a coincidence? It seemed unlikely.

"Can you increase the resolution?" Jacinta asked.

"Not on a static image. Give me a minute."

8:17

Jacinta was used to Lindel not explaining everything she did. She only put up with the habit because she knew she wouldn't understand half of any given explanation the young genius would offer, even if asked. A minute later a new image of the star field came up, shifting, so it centred around a small blank spot in the screen.

"I've hooked into the NASA database so we can get a clearer picture of the region. As you can see, Dr. Raynolds was correct. This dark spot here should be where Sirius A can be seen." She tapped some commands into the computer and used the mouse to drag the image in a circle until it faced almost ninety degrees from where it had been.

Jacinta pursed her lips as the drawing aligned with the image.

"If this drawing is supposed to represent the sky, what are all these other dots?"

Lindel thought for a moment before pulling up yet another image.

"This is archived footage from a Hubble deep field scan of the region."

She rotated the image again and sat back for an instant before adjusting the transparency of the drawing and overlaying the two.

"She knew," Jacinta whispered. "But how..?"

"Simple," Lindel returned. "Whoever we have in that cell is no seven-year-old girl. She's not Sarah at all. None of them are."

CHAPTER 17

Two and a half minutes later, Director Illum was standing at Lindel's desk looking as pole-axed as Jacinta had felt a moment before.

"With me," he said, a look of deep anger struggling to work its way onto his normally impassive face.

Jacinta fell in behind her boss with no doubt as to his destination. When they reached Sarah's cell, he didn't even acknowledge the tech monitoring her, simply opening the door and striding in. He sat in the only adult sized seat while Jacinta moved towards the corner, the door closing automatically behind her.

Sarah took one look at his impatient form and came to sit on the other side of the low desk. Bright crayons worn down to various lengths lay strewn across its surface.

"Did you like my drawing, Director Illum?" She asked innocently.

"Enough… I'm not even going to call you Sarah. Whoever you really are, enough."

The young girl nodded, causing part of her long blonde hair to fall across her shoulder.

"You worked it out, didn't you? You know," she said shrewdly.

"I know you're not Sarah Winthrop, regardless of what our best information says. I know you drew us a star map three days ago. I know it has a region blanked out that corresponds to an abnormality our best minds and technology have only just now discovered. And I know that you're not trying to harm us."

Jacinta perked up at that. What had made Director Illum say that last part? Something in her mind made the connection, and she gave a small involuntary gasp.

The nuclear fuel rods as a power source. The weapons pointing upwards despite a straight-line beam system. An object heading towards them from space.

These people, whoever they were, weren't terrorists, or even enemies. They were building a clandestine defence network across every landmass on earth. And she and thousands of others like her around the globe had been dismantling their efforts as rapidly as possible.

8:17

"If our plans had been successful, that is more than you would have had to know. Tomorrow you would have seen dozens of beams of light shoot from various points on your planet, lasting for precisely three-point-seven-two seconds. In the aftermath you would then find the slagged remains of our machines, with no discernible clues as to their origin. Unfortunately, your people are both stubborn and tenacious, and our best efforts with your limited technology have proven only partially successful."

Director Illum squeezed his eyes shut for a moment as he rubbed his face before taking a deep breath and returning to calmness.

"My name is Jeff Illum, Director of the Australian Anti-Terrorist Unit. Whom am I addressing?"

Sarah smiled in what appeared to be a genuine emotion. One of the first Jacinta had ever seen from her. Sarah stared at the director for a long time, weighing her response.

"I suppose it no longer matters. One way or another we can no longer avoid interfering in your planet's affairs. I am Hially, Captain of the Eradicator, the ship my people are based on.

"Your people? What… species, are you?"

The creature masquerading as Sarah smiled again.

"There are forty-seven distinct species on my crew Director, but that is a conversation for another time. What you should be focusing on in the seven hours your planet has left is completing the few machines we could not initialize due to material shortages."

"I can't authorise that," Illum told her flatly.

"Then I suggest you find someone who can. *Your* species depends on it."

"What is the bare minimum number of machines you need to destroy the object?"

"If I were to bet, I would say three clean shots should do it. But this is not something you want to bet on."

"So five then?" Illum pushed.

"That should be effective if activated before the mass reaches Earth's orbit."

"And where will it hit? Do you have coordinates? No, of course you don't. Otherwise you wouldn't have had to build these things all over the planet."

Sarah, Hially, whoever she really was, nodded. "Correct, we won't have a final landing site until the mass rounds the moon and clears its gravity well."

"Wait. A landing site? Not an impact site?" Jeff said almost to himself.

Jacinta felt her blood run cold at the ramifications of that minor difference in words.

"I've told you all I can, Director Illum. If the machines do their job, that is all you will ever need to know. Believe me, you don't want the rest of your life plagued by the nightmares that will come if I am required to reveal to you the last piece of this puzzle."

Jeff looked her in the eye for a long, measuring moment before standing. "Thank you for the warning, Captain Hially. I need to confer with my superiors."

The young girl stood as well, nodded as he left, hands behind her back. This wasn't the pose of a lying seven-year-old, more like a military officer dismissing an underling so they could go about their task.

Jacinta stayed a moment longer, a million questions running through her mind. She figured she would only get one.

"Why are you going to such lengths to help us? You don't owe our people anything."

"Our motives are anything but altruistic. If we can eradicate the threat without your world being destroyed we will do so, we are not barbarians. But if any part of the mass reaches the surface, your world will be lost before my ships can arrive. At that point we will do what is required to stop it spreading further."

Hially moved a sheet of paper out from underneath the pile of crayons and lifted a scrap from beneath. On it were four glyphs in the same style as the images Seth had sent back from Perth before his death.

There was a circle with a line through it. An isosceles triangle with the thin wedge pointing northeast. Something that looked like an upside down 'e'. And finally, what looked like a cylinder cut diagonally on both ends so you could see the interior.

"What is this?" Jacinta asked with a frown.

"Keep it. If you survive the next two days, it might come in handy."

And just like that, they were back to playing games.

CHAPTER 18

An hour had passed since Sarah, or Hially if she were to be believed, had delivered her message. It had sounded like truth at the time, and Jacinta wanted to believe her, but they had been down this road too many times with the awakened.

She couldn't help thinking about the boy who cried wolf. Was this just another elaborate deception? Or had they finally come to some portion of the truth to explain all the mayhem these people had caused over the last several months? And if so, despite their appearance, were the awakened even people at all?

As she approached Director Illum's office she could hear raised voices, and Jameson was stationed outside his door in full tactical gear.

"Sorry ma'am, no one is to interrupt," he said seriously as she closed the distance. Jacinta raised an eyebrow and attempted to sidestep the man, who, while being a highly experienced and trained operative, was still her subordinate.

Jameson took a sideways step, and she ran into him when he refused to back down.

"Sorry, Jacinta. Orders from the Director."

She stared at him icily for a moment, then relented. If Jeff had given the order, Jameson was just doing his job. It also meant the director considered whatever he was dealing with more important than receiving potential updates in real time. That was not something the director Made a habit of.

The yelling from the office was getting louder, the words almost legible from behind the thick glass. There was a moment of silence, then the door flung open, and Director Illum took a half step out. He saw the two of them waiting, and nodded as if he'd expected nothing less.

"Both of you. My office."

Jameson raised an eyebrow when Jacinta gave him a small grin of triumph, but they headed in without a word and sat opposite the director at his desk.

"Given the now overwhelming evidence that these people are not just coma patients who have woken under mysterious circumstances, coupled with the very real threat this spaceborne object presents, I've convinced the Prime Minister that we need to assist the awakened in completing their machines. But General Blake is not happy," he said without preamble. "He is insisting that only military personnel be involved. The long story short is that our orders are to coordinate the awakened. They'll act as advisors while military personnel carry out the actual work and operate the machines when the time comes."

"That sounds messy," Jacinta replied.

"More than you know. For right now, go back to Sarah and get the location of any machines we missed, and start Lindel coordinating whatever parts and materials we'll need onsite. Jameson, I want three agents on every awakened released into the field. You'll personally see to Sarah… Captain Hially's, safety."

"Sir," Jameson acknowledged.

"Have Mike coordinate with General Blake once you have the locations of the remaining machines, his engineers will meet you onsite."

The director sighed.

"Make no mistake, I still don't trust these people as far as I can throw them. But the alternative is to do nothing while an object hurtles towards us on a collision course from space. If nothing else they've said is true, we know that part is, and that we don't have the space defence capabilities to stop it."

"Understood Sir, we'll get it done," Jacinta told him.

* * *

By the time the army engineers were in place and the work underway, there was less than four hours left until the object rounded the moon. Deep space telescopes had been trained on the mass, but as yet, it was too far away to get more than a blurry visual of a roughly ovoid shape. Spectral imaging still refused to identify the object's composition.

To say that she'd been shocked when Jeff had asked Sarah outright for the locations of any remaining machines, and she'd complied, would be a massive understatement. Captain Hially had simply added that double crossing the awakened at this point would only ensure humanity's destruction, but the choice was now theirs to make.

As it turned out, the A.T.U. had entirely missed one of the weapons constructed in an abandoned mine shaft outside Coober Pedy. It was the only one in the country which was fully functional.

Several more had been captured in raids but never finished, and a few destroyed as the awakened had lost their positions and lives in the process.

8:17

There was a second machine outside Freemantle on the west coast which was close to completion. Hopes were high that it could be made functional by the time the object rounded the moon.

Right now Jacinta was standing in a warehouse not fifteen blocks from A.T.U. headquarters here in Sydney where another machine was being feverishly constructed by an army of antlike workers. Every one of them scrambling to assemble the unfamiliar equipment according to the awakened's specifications before the deadline.

To her right, Victoria, or whoever was pretending to be Victoria, barked frustrated orders at a group of technicians. Other awakened were busy working on the software interface under close guard.

General Blake was also onsite, trying desperately to control a situation he had no way of understanding at short notice. She wished he would just go back to the base. His presence here was not speeding up the process, and they could ill afford the delays his constant questioning was creating.

This machine differed from the others. It was bereft of the exoskeleton which had first tipped them off that something unusual was happening with the awakened. Without its housing, this one was around half the size, and Sarah refused to guarantee it would even work.

Even if it did, once activated, the radiation spillage would be significant. Blake had tried to veto the whole idea, but had been overruled by the minister for defence. In frustration, the General now had soldiers lining the factory with as much lead plating as they could rig up at short notice and spraying it all down with fast drying concrete. Sarah agreed it 'might' help, and Jacinta hoped she wasn't just patronising the General to give him something to do.

Two other machines in Brisbane and Darwin were also being worked on by now, but it was unlikely they would be completed in time.

Sarah had said they didn't want to gamble with a lack of firepower. Right at this moment, with machine parts all over the floor of the warehouse, it seemed like it would take a miracle even to get that far.

* * *

Three hours later, as a crane moved the last piece of superstructure into place, they received confirmation that the machine in Freemantle had been completed.

"Two down," Jacinta said nervously.

Sarah shook her head.

8:17

"It's not enough."

"What will it take to guarantee success?" Jacinta asked as she stared at the mass of activity across the warehouse.

Sarah? Hially? looked at her for a long moment before sighing just like any normal seven-year-old might.

"Less water," she eventually replied.

Jacinta frowned for a moment before understanding.

"Earth has too much water. If any part of the mass makes it into an ocean, your planet is doomed.

"And your machines can only be built on land," Jacinta added.

The young girl nodded. "At least with this level of technology. We had hoped to send some out on freighter ships, but due to your obstinate resistance we ran out of time and resources."

"Forgive me for saying so, but this doesn't seem like a very well-planned operation for people with access to your level of technology."

Sarah looked at her, unimpressed, but eventually relented.

"Your people have a saying. Plan B. This is more like plan D."

"Oh," was all Jacinta could come up with. "What was plan A?"

"For established countermeasures to prevent this from ever occurring again."

"Does *this* happen often?" Jacinta tried again.

"Images coming in," Lindel interrupted from the table beside them.

Jacinta and Sarah moved towards her so they could see the screen as well.

A moment later a high-resolution image of the moon's edge appeared, obviously taken by satellite as there was no atmospheric blurring.

"Magnifying sector G8," Lindel announced without prompting.

The image closed to a small portion of the original off to the right of the moon's surface, centring on an object that was still hard to define.

"Can you go in closer?" Jacinta asked.

"Yes, the resolution of the original is sufficient."

Jacinta nodded and Lindel zoomed in as far as she could on the offending object.

"That's no asteroid. What is that?!" Lindel whispered, a look of horror on her face at the amorphous blob the screen had revealed.

Jacinta could only imagine how she herself must look right now, eyes wide, hands clenched until the blood ran away from them.

"That," a small voice said from beside them. "Is the great enemy, and unless we can immolate it beyond its ability to regenerate, it will consume your world within days."

CHAPTER 19

"I think you'd better elaborate on that," General Blake said as came over to where they were standing, apparently he'd been close enough to overhear Hially's previous statement.

The girl looked up at him and then back at Jacinta, who nodded for her to continue.

"We had hoped to spare you from the burden of this knowledge at your current level of development. In that we have failed. What you are seeing is a macro virus, engineered by a foolish race who thought it could win them a war almost fifteen hundred of your years ago."

She took a breath.

Jacinta could barely comprehend those words coming from the innocent face of a seven-year-old.

"They were right. Their weapon won the war in a day, then it killed them as well. Within a week nothing was left of their planet but a lifeless husk, and tens of billions of virus cells. Within a month, the virus had spread to the point where every conceivable resource on the surface was used up. But a virus' primary function is always to continue to replicate."

"How did it get off their planet?" Blake asked intently.

"It learned, adapted, mutated until it resembled something more like a colony of ants than a typical virus. It has developed many specialised functions over the centuries, some of which allow it to launch itself into interstellar space. Even to defend itself against ballistic attack."

"So you're saying our missiles will not be effective?"

Sarah just shook her head.

They had received word through official channels less than an hour ago that America, Russia, and China were all preparing nuclear assaults. They would launch as soon as the mass' post moon trajectory could be calculated.

"Nothing at your level of technology will be effective against the mass except a nuclear bomb."

"Many of the warheads we're sending towards it *are* nuclear," Blake said with a satisfied grin.

"Yes," Hially answered sadly. "But their delivery mechanisms are far more primitive. They will never get close enough to detonate in effective range before the mass eliminates them."

"Then we'll send more," Blake announced as if it were a simple solution.

"A mass this size can propel its outer cells forward as countermeasures. Can you send millions of missiles? Because it will not hesitate to sacrifice millions of cells to make landfall on a resource rich planet like Earth."

Blake's hairline moved back slightly as his eyebrows rose.

"No."

"Neither could anyone else. The enemy spread out from its own system like fire, exponentially reaching more and more planets. Some barren, others teaming with life. It has no regard for anything we hold dear. It desires only to consume. By the time it reached a race known as the Syringa's borders, it had already consumed thousands of systems. Thankfully, the Syringa were a highly advanced spacefaring civilisation. They were also intelligent enough to know that holing up inside their own borders would only mean the mass would eventually surround them and keep coming at them, forever. They fought for centuries against the enemy, making allies where they could, protecting what races and planets they could. But in the end even their homeworld fell."

"What happened?" Lindel asked in horror.

"Space is vast," Sarah responded. "The enemy doesn't care about our conceptual ideas of distance and direction. They attacked the Syringa from every star system within a hundred light years on all three axes. It was a coordinated attack of unprecedented proportions, but at that time the mass had grown large enough that it could think at that level. The Syringa held out for a week, then another, but the enemy had sent billions of individual spores into their space. Each designed to house and protect a single viable cell. That's all it takes. If the cell goes unnoticed for an hour or two, it will have already multiplied. Within a day there are too many to stop."

Jacinta shuddered. "How many do you think are in the mass approaching us?"

Hially studied the image and sighed. "It's just a guess, but probably close to a million viable cells plus the dead outer structure."

"So we really can't stop it?" Jacinta asked quietly.

Sarah just shook her head. "No, but we can. Before the Syringa empire fell, they had created a vast military. When they lost their last remaining planet, these homeless ships took on a new mission. They spread out throughout the galaxy with a singular purpose. Warn every race even close to a level of technology which could help, and give them the tools to defend themselves with. Thus was the Confederation born."

"The Confederation?" Lindel asked, more fascinated that horrified at Hially's words.

Sarah nodded. "Thousands of races, over twenty thousand planets at its height. The Confederation was a desperate alliance of every species that could be convinced, bribed or compelled to help stem the tide. It took them almost eight hundred of your years, and the loss of over two thousand of the Confederation's species to win that war, but eventually they were victorious; the great enemy burned away from every world it was found on. When the war was finally over, the boundless survey began. It took almost another hundred years, but in every star system in the galaxy there is now a beacon. Each one is keyed to activate if it senses even a single cell of the enemy, dormant or otherwise."

"And ours activated," Jacinta said thoughtfully.

"We had thought them gone forever. Over fifty years have passed since the last activation. But this mass seems to have been travelling all this time between the arms of the galaxy towards the Orion

Spur. We always assumed there could be some cells out there that were still viable. But that a mass this size could still be active and have avoided detection for so long? Well, let's say this information has shaken a great many people."

"So you were sent to destroy it? To stop it spreading again."

Hially nodded. "I command a group of eighty dreadnoughts tasked with eradicating this mass and all component parts it might spawn. We will arrive at your planet in time to stop this mass reaching space borne capability, if barely. I sincerely regret that due to the vast distances involved, we will not arrive until it is too late to save your people."

"Are you telepathic then?" Lindel asked abruptly.

"Not naturally," Hially said with a small smile. "But we possess technology which allows us to enter the mind of another if they choose not to resist."

"That's why you targeted the comatose patients. It was never them at all, was it? You've been in control all along," Jacinta blurted out as the realisation hit her.

The young girl nodded. "It was not easy, or safe, combining that technology with our communications arrays to send the signal over light years. There were several accidents, but as I said before, this was more like plan D. Those who died, did so knowing what was at stake, not only for your world, but for their own if the mass got out of control."

"I'm sorry," Jacinta found herself saying.

The young girl's brows furrowed, not understanding.

"On behalf of the A.T.U., I'm sorry for your people that we killed in our raids. We didn't know… We thought you were trying to do us harm," Jacinta said quietly.

Hially nodded seriously.

"We know that, and I thank you for your sentiment, however it is unnecessary. Those operatives were simply cut off from the bodies they were controlling, they are not dead. You owe your apologies to the families of their hosts if anyone. We had intended to return them to you once our task was complete. That will not be possible for those who are no longer alive."

Jacinta felt as though someone had punched her in the guts. She sat heavily in a nearby chair. Everything they'd believed about the awakened had been wrong. Not just a little off target, but blindly, polar-opposite wrong. It had all made sense along the way, but she had been the one to authorise those raids, she had coordinated with military units to carry them out. How many families would curse her name when this was all done, when they saw other awakened reunited, properly this time, with their loved ones?

"A small enough price to pay," Hially assured her. "If we succeed, their sacrifice will be the salvation of your world."

"And if we fail?" Blake asked.

"Then they'll be a few days ahead of the rest of humanity."

CHAPTER 20

"It's time," General Blake announced from across the room.

Director Illum looked up and nodded before coming over to the table where Jacinta, Hially, and Lindel were standing.

"I'm heading to the command centre with General Blake to monitor the situation and provide tactical support. We should have a final track on the mass' trajectory in little over half an hour. You're in command of this onsite task force now Jacinta. The General has ordered his officers to obey your orders. Get it finished, and I'll see you on the other side."

She nodded gravely.

"So, no pressure then."

Jeff gave her a rueful smile as he walked away, joining General Blake before the pair of them headed towards a waiting car.

"Will we be ready in time?" she asked Hially once the director had left.

The alien captain in the young girl's form looked across the warehouse at Victoria, who somehow sensed it and nodded back.

"Yes, but that only matters if the mass touches down somewhere in this part of the Pacific. Anywhere else and one of my other teams around your world will have to make the shot."

"What's the best-case scenario?" Jacinta prompted.

Hially thought for a moment, or at least, got that far-away look the way she sometimes did.

"If it heads towards southern Africa, we should be able to eliminate it shortly after it rounds the moon. Our defences there are all but complete."

"And the worst case?"

"That's easy, anywhere at sea."

"They can survive a landing in open water?" Lindel asked.

"They prefer it. It causes less damage to the outer shell, meaning more cells survive to begin consuming the biomass of your oceans. With seabeds as deep as Earth's, you lack the technology to resist even a single cell entering at speed."

"I don't understand," Lindel responded. "You keep talking about how a single cell can destroy a world. They can't be that powerful."

"You're correct, a single cell is no great threat on its own, and no bigger than a metre across. The problem comes when that cell has time to reproduce."

"It's time you told us exactly what we're facing," Jacinta told her.

Hially nodded. "Very well. The moment the cell enters your ocean it will begin consuming biomass in the form of plankton, fish, even the water itself. By day two it will have split into a hundred copies of itself. By day three, the pattern will continue and there will now be ten thousand, give or take a few casualties. On day four, a million. Day five, a hundred million cells will scour the seafloor, consuming everything in their path and probably finding their way back to land. On day six, there will be a billion cells. Day seven, a hundred billion, on day eight, ten trillion. Of course, by that time your entire biosphere will be gone, your ocean consumed and dried up. Every surface of the planet will be covered in cells like a coat of algae dozens of metres deep. By day nine, the mass will have reached a critical point where it will have enough connections to begin thinking at a far more complex level. It will then begin forming the structures which will allow it to return to space and begin the infection anew."

Jacinta just stood there, her jaw slack. What did one say to the calmly mapped out destruction of one's entire world?

"When will your ships arrive?" Lindel stuttered.

Hially looked at the ground for a moment before answering.

"No earlier than day six. Unfortunately, those numbers were projected on a single cell. If a hundred make it into your ocean, or worse, ten thousand survive, that projection jumps forward a day or two. If we fail, and the mass makes ocean fall unimpeded, my ships will arrive on day ten of that projection. At that time we will hunt down any cells already launched and bombard the mass on the surface from orbit. We will continue until the entire planetary crust is nothing but super-heated plasma."

Jacinta felt like she was going to throw up. This couldn't be happening. It was like something out of a science-fiction movie. Whether it was a meteor smashing into Earth, or an alien race razing humanity's monuments and cities, those movies rarely turned out well for the everyday people of planet Earth.

Gripping the edge of the table, she forced herself to relative calmness.

"What can we do?" She asked quietly.

Hially just jutted her chin at the work proceeding across the factory.

"Everything that can be done, is being done. In a few minutes we'll know the mass' final trajectory. Until then, all we can do is wait."

Jacinta took a deep breath and sat down in a chair nearby.

"If we kill enough of them, will you be able to save us?"

Hially just shook her head.

"I'm sorry. Once the infection takes hold, a planet is doomed. If by some miracle you can keep its numbers low for a day or two, we may reach you in time to do some good. My ships can take several thousand survivors on board, but only if we can find an area the enemy hasn't yet spread to. I know it's not much, but if you can put up a staunch enough resistance, your species may yet survive."

Jacinta nodded. "You're right, that's not much. We'll just have to make this work."

CHAPTER 21

Half an hour later, Director Illum and General Blake arrived at the command centre. Jacinta had filled them in on the full details of what they were facing and both men had gone silent while she relayed what Sarah had told her. Since there was nothing they could do about it right now, however, the plan for the next hour remained the same.

The machine was close to finished. The structure was in place and the army of engineers and awakened were frantically completing the wiring and control interface under Victoria's less than patient eye. A dozen soldiers off to the side were guarding the transport containers housing the four nuclear fuel rods which would power it once complete.

Director Illum was on the line from the command centre at the base, and everyone was on edge. The next hour would hopefully see a few bright lines of light reach for the sky, with most of the world oblivious as to their intent. Either that, or it would mark the beginning of the end for humanity.

"Jacinta, are you there?" Director Illum said over the comm. link.

"Yes sir, you're on with myself, Lindel Harding, and Captain Hially."

"Good, the Prime Minister just briefed me on global preparedness and the news is not good. Less than thirty percent of the planet's surface will have sufficient weapons coverage to eliminate the threat. Less than ten percent has redundancy."

"That's not good," Lindel muttered.

"No. The Americans, Russians, and Chinese are launching shuttles within the hour. If all else fails, they'll dock with the I.S.S. and attempt to hold out until Captain Hially's armada arrives."

"We're not there yet," Jacinta said.

"We are. By the time the mass reaches the ground it will be too late. If it hits the ocean, its impact will cause a tidal wave large enough to cause significant flooding on most coasts around the world. Even if it makes landfall, it will create enough atmospheric disturbance on the way down to significantly lower the chances of a successful launch after the fact."

"Here we go," Lindel said as she studied her

monitor where a direct uplink to the NASA satellite data was being displayed.

Jacinta looked at her, then at the screen full of numbers which she had no idea how to interpret.

There was also a graphic representation of the mass as it began rounding the moon. In truth, she trusted Lindel to keep her updated via the real-time data far more than she did a pixelated graphic.

"The mass is beginning to round the moon. At this rate it will take approximately thirty-eight seconds until we can determine a post-orbit trajectory and extrapolate a landing site."

"Javary, how long?" Hially called down to the floor.

"More than five minutes, less than ten," the being pretending to be Victoria called back.

Javary. So that was her real name. Was the creature even a her? Jacinta suddenly thought. And how did she know it had been the same alien, person, connected with Victoria's body this whole time?

Jacinta pushed the unhelpful thoughts out of her head. None of that mattered now, just the stream of numbers cascading down the screen which Lindel was glued to.

"Make your calculations quick, but make them right," Hially called back.

The being pretending to be Victoria nodded back and began checking over the work which had already been done.

Jacinta could do nothing but count the seconds as each passed interminably by. She wanted to scream in frustration. The world might very well be ending, and all she could do was stand here and wait for the news that, yes, they were doomed. Or not.

"Ten seconds till orbital exit," Lindel announced.

Jacinta had the sudden insane urge to count each one down, new year's style, and had to catch herself before she let a giggle escape. It was just the stress, it had to be.

At least Lindel had something to do.

"Post-orbital trajectory achieved," Lindel announced. "Calculating landing vector now."

Jacinta found herself holding her breath, and had to force herself to calmness, or something close to it. Thirty percent. No gambler in their right mind would take those odds.

Lindel sat back, her face ashen.

"What are we looking at?" Jacinta demanded.

8:17

"It's on us," Lindel said quietly.

"So it's coming down within our weapons range?"

Jacinta asked.

"Yes, very much so."

"What do you mean?"

Hially looked at the numbers on the screen, pulled up the set of coordinates on another screen, and paled slightly.

"It's in our weapon range all right, but it's coming in over water, about twenty kilometres that way," Sarah said, pointing at the eastern wall of the warehouse.

"If we don't stop it, in a little over two hours it's going to make ocean fall about two kilometres into Sydney harbour."

CHAPTER 22

"Ready to fire," Victoria called up to them just under ten minutes later.

Hially nodded her permission.

Victoria moved to the console under the watchful eye of a guard who wouldn't be able to tell from the readouts even if she were trying something dubious. All the controls were in that same language found on the machine Seth had died trying to disarm.

"So that's it? We can kill it?"

Sarah shook her head slightly.

"Maybe. Maybe we shouldn't try. At least not right away."

"What are you talking about?" Jacinta responded a little too loudly.

Sarah squinted a little in concentration as she studied the readouts.

"You'll remember I told you that three of our

machines would be the minimum required to stop it?"

Jacinta nodded. "Are you saying it won't be enough?"

"There was always that chance. That's why I specified it as a minimum. If the enemy was over land, I wouldn't need to suggest this. If over water, we would have no choice but to try, and hope. With its touchdown coordinates so close to land though, we might be able to hit it with a glancing blow with the emplacement on the west coast and redirect it onto a landfall trajectory. We could then hit it with the final two emplacements on the east coast as it enters the atmosphere."

"Why not just blow it to pieces now?" General Blake asked over the comm link.

"Because that's exactly what we don't want," Sarah replied flatly. "There may be millions of cells in that mass. If even a small chunk breaks off and preserves a single viable cell long enough to make ocean fall, any chance of your species surviving this is over."

"But how would a glancing blow help?" Lindel asked from beside her. "Wouldn't that just tear open the outer structure and spill countless cells into the atmosphere?"

"It would, if we waited until it got to the atmosphere," Sarah said with a small smile.

Lindel nodded. "Yes, of course."

Jacinta raised an eyebrow in demand for an explanation.

"The outer layer is made of dead cells, exposed to the vacuum of space," Sarah explained when she saw Jacinta hadn't understood. "The same cells form the interior. You see these protrusions here, and here?" she asked, pointing at the high-resolution image of the mass as it approached the Earth.

Jacinta nodded.

"They function as flaps when a mass enters the atmosphere, slowing its descent and ensuring it doesn't burn up on re-entry. The enemy is horrifying in its destructive capability, but still subject to the same laws of physics as the rest of us. An uncontrolled entry would create enough friction that it would break apart and mostly burn up before it made landfall."

"But some would still make it to the ground?" Blake interjected.

"The probability is high. However, if we attack before it enters the atmosphere, any spillage will freeze in space and become inert before it becomes a problem. Of course, the mass will compensate, plugging the hole with cells until it regains an airtight seal. But by then the escaping atmosphere will have acted as a primitive thruster, knocking it further onto a trajectory of our choosing."

"How far can we alter its flight path?" Director Illum added from the comm. "Are we able to move it away from populated centres?"

"Unlikely, due to the overpopulated nature of the region," Hially responded after a moment. "How far we can alter its course will depend on how much atmosphere is expelled during the attack. It will also depend on how quickly the mass can stem the leak. At a rough guess, we could gain anywhere from five kilometres to fifty. The sooner we act, the greater effect the trajectory change will have. Either way, the only factor that matters at this moment is that it doesn't make contact with the ocean."

"How can you say that? How can you expect us to intentionally redirect a crashing alien invader into a city of millions, and say that doesn't matter?"

Hially grimaced. "It matters, General. Just not when compared to the seven and a half billion lives that will be lost if we don't act, and any part of the mass touches down in the harbour."

"You're asking me to authorise an action which will lead to the destruction of our most densely populated city. To sacrifice our citizens in order to save countries that would conquer us in a moment if they thought they could get away with it."

"I'm asking you to save your species," Hially returned.

"We didn't come to your world to save this country, or even the human race. My orders are to destroy the enemy before it can spread again and consume anything more than a single world. Everything we have done as what you have termed, 'the awakened' has been above and beyond those orders. An action I initiated once we discovered we could telepathically connect with some members of your species."

There were several seconds of silence over the comms and then Blake made a strangled reply.

"I can't authorise that. Only the Prime Minister can make that call."

"Then I suggest you get that dealt with, and begin evacuating the city," Hially replied.

"I take it the rest of you understand why we need to do this?" she pointedly asked.

Lindel nodded, while Jeff issued a sullen 'yes' over the comms. Jacinta nodded sadly.

"Intellectually we do. But you're talking about hundreds of thousands of deaths at best, probably millions. That's a hard sacrifice to accept for our people."

Hially nodded. "Yes. I've seen some of what you call movies since I've been here. I find it interesting that many of them have a commonality, that at the last moment something unexpected occurs, and everything turns out alright in the end. It points to something odd in your psyche, though I cannot tell if it is the worst kind of naivety, or the inability to conceive of defeat."

"Perhaps it's a little of both," Jacinta returned. "We don't give up easily."

"I understand. No species stands at the brink and then knowingly steps over. However, as I already told you, this enemy has claimed thousands of worlds. Most of those species were far more technologically advanced and prepared than you are. If you don't do everything in your power to stop it, it will consume you and your world, and move on. And it will not care that it did so."

They lapsed into an uncomfortable silence until a few minutes later the comms came alive once more with the sound of General Blake's voice.

"The Prime Minister will address the nation momentarily. In the meantime, he has authorised me to tell you to carry out your plan. It seems he agrees with you about the larger picture. I don't. I gave an oath to protect the people of this country, not the rest of the world. You're asking me to perform an action that could lead to up to ten percent casualties of our total population. I won't do it. I told the Prime Minister the same, and he demanded my immediate resignation. Therefore I have informed him I will cede my position and rank per his orders, but I will not leave my post until the evacuation is complete. This is on your consciences now. Blake out."

The three women sat and stood completely still for a moment, absorbing what they'd just heard.

"Lindel, get to work. Captain Hially, if you don't mind?"

The girl nodded and moved over next to Lindel, where they began computing the new firing solution. Even if they succeeded in altering the mass' trajectory away from the ocean, it was unlikely they could avoid the city altogether. The casualties would be immense. But the alternative was far worse, so she forced herself to stand silently by whilst they continued.

It took a few minutes, but finally Lindel and Hially came to an agreement.

"We have it," Lindel announced. "We'll need to fire the machine in western Australia in six minutes and fourteen seconds to achieve the optimal firing angle."

8:17

Jacinta nodded at them both. "Get on it."

The following six minutes were the longest of Jacinta's life. The world was ending, or near enough to it. She should have something to do. But the orders had been given, the preparations made, and the higher-up's informed. All she could do was wait, and pace as she monitored the evacuation on the comm feeds, which was only now beginning in earnest. The national emergency broadcast system had taken over all T.V. and radio stations. The Prime Minister was busy telling everybody to get as far away from central Sydney as quickly as they could. Within minutes there would be mass panic, closely followed by impassable congestion on every road.

Those on the outskirts of the city might make it, those closer in had no chance of escaping. As Hially had observed, the vastly overpopulated maze of streets and canals which comprised the inner-city's urban sprawl precluded all chance of a quick escape. By the time the clock wound down to zero, the PM's message was on its third rotation.

"Firing," Hially announced calmly, as if the fate of the world didn't depend on the next few seconds. Jacinta wanted to shout at her out of pure frustration, but even she knew it wouldn't help. Instead, she leaned in closer to the high-resolution feed still aimed at the mass.

"Come on," she whispered. "Come on."

There was a flash of green barely a second long, then the satisfying sight of gases being expelled from the mass' side. Thousands upon thousands of what she assumed to be individual cells ejected out with that gas, appearing as little more than motes of dust even at this level of magnification.

The mass tilted off its axis, rotating just enough to reveal the wound in its side already beginning to close. There appeared no hesitation by the mass to sacrifice even more of itself to reform the outer shell. The cells settled into position along the tear and immediately froze, the surrounding cold of the vacuum claiming them as they hardened into place.

Soon enough it was done, and the mass was once again whole. If it weren't for the cloud of inert cells still floating around it, there would have been no way to tell an attack had even occurred.

"Recalculating trajectory," Lindel announced.

Jacinta couldn't help tapping her foot impatiently, but the last thing she wanted to do right now was distract the analyst from doing her job.

"Got it. It's not good."

"Where will it land?" Jacinta demanded.

"The good news is we succeeded. It's on land. The

bad news is that we only shifted it about ten kilometres southwest. It's going to make landfall in an industrial estate near Sydney Park. Approximately two point eight kilometres from the southern end of the central business district."

"How far from water is it?" Hially added a moment later.

"Checking. Whatever part of the mass survives our next attack should hit approximately four kilometres from the water to the north, and almost the same to the south." Lindel frowned. "There is a canal nearby which provides much easier, if longer, access in that direction."

"Send that to Blake and Jeff," Jacinta ordered without hesitation.

A long moment went by as Lindel sent the information to the main control room at the base, where Director Illum and General Blake's replacement were overseeing the operation.

"That sounds close to your location," Jeff's voice said over the channel, making Jacinta's ears prick up.

"Yes Sir, things here could get a little… bumpy," Lindel replied.

"Are we in danger?" Jacinta asked.

Lindel thought for a long moment, but slowly shook her head.

"We'll feel the impact for certain, but we should be far enough away that the structure protects us from any residual shockwave. Remember, it's more or less hollow inside, it won't hit with anywhere near the force of, say, a meteor of the same size. More like a mammoth downed aircraft, minus the combustible fuel. It doesn't use combustible fuel, does it?" she asked Hially abruptly.

"No, nor radioactive materials. Its goal is to make landfall intact, not kill itself if something goes wrong."

Lindel nodded, somewhat reassured, and Jacinta took a deep, calming breath.

"Captain Hially, this is General Huon," a fresh voice said over the secure comm. link. "We're preparing to scramble all available aircraft to neutralise any remaining cells once the mass touches down. Do you have any advice as to what type of ordinance will be most effective?"

"Yes General, forget bullets and explosives. What you want is to burn the mass at a temperature of over three thousand degrees centigrade for no less than two point three seconds. Anything less may not be effective."

8:17

"Understood. Thank you Captain."

The comm went dead again and Lindel turned to face them.

"That doesn't leave us many options, and almost none for a ground defence."

"At your level of technology, no," Hially responded.

"How long until we fire the remaining machines?" Jacinta asked nervously.

Lindel checked the screen before turning towards her.

"The mass will enter the atmosphere in forty-three minutes. We'll fire ten seconds after it hits atmospheric turbulence to ensure the friction hasn't altered its course."

"And then we'll see if the human race survives," Jacinta said to herself.

CHAPTER 23

Forty-two minutes had passed since Lindel's announcement, and they were as ready as they could be for the looming apocalypse. Every plane that could be scrambled was in the air, loaded with munitions which would hopefully mop up any cells which survived the impact.

Word had just reached them that the combined nuclear strike had failed, just as Hially had predicted it would. In response, both the U.S. and China had dispatched elite military units to deal with the existential threat. All warnings from the Australian government about international borders and sovereign airspace had been ignored by both superpowers. In any event, on the short notice they'd all had since the mass' final landing coordinates had been determined, it didn't look like either force would arrive in time to do anything but create a massive international incident. If anyone survived this day to care about it.

8:17

"The mass will contact the mesosphere in ten seconds," Lindel announced.

"Prepare to fire," Hially called down to Victoria, who was personally operating the massive machine at the other end of the warehouse.

Jacinta still couldn't bring herself to like the woman who had taunted her for months as they'd chased the awakened around the city.

They had been so desperate to prevent this exact moment, this firing of unknown weapons with their unknown targets, and every step she had taken to prevent it had seemed correct at the time. Looking back though, Jacinta could only clench her fists and hope that her efforts in stopping the awakened hadn't been successful enough that the entire world was about to pay the price.

"Contact," Lindel announced, and on her screen the mass started to glow a deep cherry red as it entered the friction of Earth's outer atmosphere.

"Confirm trajectory," Jacinta ordered.

"A few more seconds," Lindel replied.

Jacinta wanted to scream for lack of something to do. Long seconds passed by as Lindel just stared at her screen, outwardly appearing to do nothing while the object streaked towards Earth.

The mass began to glow brighter as it contacted the stratosphere, and Lindel nodded to herself.

"Confirming trajectory."

The screen displayed a series of equations which were lost on Jacinta, but Lindel and Hially nodded to each other.

"Sync cannons to established coordinates and fire when ready," Hially called to Victoria.

"Trajectory and landing site confirmed, no surprises," Lindel announced.

Victoria finished whatever needed doing at the console of the machine and nodded back towards them.

"Here we go," Hially said. "Don't look at the beam."

Down at the machine, Victoria was yelling the same instructions to the engineers and other personnel still onsite.

"Firing in three, two, one…" Hially counted down.

Jacinta knew there would be no vibration from the weapon. Jameson had reported that much after the incident at the safe house. Even so, she'd expected the beam would be visible even with her eyes closed and averted.

"What happened?!" Hially all but screamed across the warehouse.

Jacinta felt a large pit open up in the bottom of her stomach as the console Victoria was standing behind blew itself apart. The machine sprayed shrapnel everywhere, killing the woman, alien, whatever she was, instantly.

"No…" was all Jacinta could manage as she realised the massive weapon had never fired.

On the screen in front of Lindel, a single green beam from the site at Coober Pedy lanced out and hit the mass, burning a hole right through it and emerging from the other side. It wasn't enough. Thousands of cells spewed out the rear of the mass, most appearing to be incinerated by the atmospheric friction. Only the slipstream created by the enormous mass still plummeting through the atmosphere kept them in check. Whether those spilled cells were viable was anybody's guess, though Hially was visibly distressed.

"Impact in fifteen seconds," Lindel announced.

"There's no time," Hially said, shaken. "The weapon looks intact, but I don't have time to rig up another interface. It's going to reach the ground."

Jacinta's mouth opened and closed as a distant roaring began to sound from all around them.

"Everybody get down and brace yourselves!" she yelled, sending the shocked personnel on the floor scurrying for cover.

"Five seconds!" Lindel yelled over the still growing noise coming from outside. Whatever else she said after that was lost as Jacinta covered her ears with her hands and crouched low to the floor.

With a cacophony she could hardly credit, the ground churned as though hit by an earthquake. Everybody left standing was thrown off their feet, and all around her large cracks appeared in the prefabricated concrete the walls were made from.

The shaking quickly subsided, but the cracks continued to grow at an alarming rate. Part of the far wall fell outwards, leading the corresponding roof section to collapse alongside it.

Men and women dived away from the collapsing structure. Some made it, others didn't. A cloud of dust and a sweeping wall of searing, dry air and dust rushed in through the gap, obscuring the cityscape beyond. Whatever remained when the dust cloud dissipated, it would not be the sight of pristine skyscrapers and the harbour bridge beyond.

She couldn't help coughing. The air was so hot and dry that it sucked all the moisture from her lungs. She crouched behind the table along with the others, and when the air had cooled enough that she could breathe normally again, she stood.

The dust was beginning to clear, revealing a grim sight beyond the wrecked wall and roof.

For as far as Jacinta could see, everything was on fire. At least, everything which had survived the initial impact.

No more than two kilometres away, the mass sat upright at an angle, squashed and damaged beyond repair on its underside. What appeared to be cracks were growing along its surface as it cooled from its descent through the atmosphere. For hundreds of metres around the crash site, nothing remained. Every factory, house, tree, and car was gone, blown away by the force of the impact. In a ring beyond the destroyed area, all that debris had been flung outward, shattering the surrounding neighbourhoods, collapsing thousands of buildings, and severely damaging those which survived. The death toll must have been immense. Even this far out, the vibrations had not left them immune. If that had been an asteroid…

Jacinta shook herself out of what she recognised as the beginnings of shock and did her best to focus. Hially and Lindel both appeared unharmed, and Jameson had appeared from somewhere to help the small girl to her feet.

"Jacinta, are you there? Jacinta!" Jeff's voice demanded over the comm.

"Fill them in," Jacinta ordered Lindel even as she turned to Hially.

"What's next? What do we do now?" she demanded after coughing up a lungful of dust.

Hially just shook her head. "I'm sorry. This is where our plan ended. There wasn't supposed to be anything left to do."

"So what, you're just going to give up? Your species might have that luxury, mine doesn't, and we're not finished yet."

Hially shook her head. "You still don't understand. The moment the outer shell of that mass cools, viable cells will pour out of the remains in the tens of thousands. You don't have the technology to combat that level of contamination."

"What about this machine? Will it still fire?"

"Even if I can rig up a new interface, we never designed them to have a firing arc that included ground targets. Our plan when we designed them never included the mass making it into the atmosphere, let alone to the ground."

Jacinta thought for a long moment in frustration. The mass was right there. She could see it through the gap in the wall, right past the most powerful weapons system on the planet. There had to be a way.

"What if we changed its angle?" Jameson asked.

"It weighs in excess of thirty tons. We have no way to do that, and no time to disassemble and reassemble it," Jacinta dismissed the idea.

"Captain Hially, how sturdy is the machine's construction?" Jameson probed.

"By human standards, extremely," the small girl replied.

"So if we were to say, collapse the floor in just the right spot to tilt the mechanism towards the mass…"

Hially gave him a grave look, but nodded slowly.

"It might work, it might break, but the weapon is currently useless how it is."

"None of this matters. The floor is solid concrete. It's one of the reasons they built it here," Lindel added, having finished debriefing the higher-ups at the base.

Jameson smiled slightly. "How many of those hand weapons do you have, Captain?"

Hially smiled a little, and Lindel's eyebrows shot up as he spoke.

"You want to use them to dig a hole which we can slide the machine into?" Jacinta asked incredulously.

"I was thinking more a rough ditch, and due to its weight the machine will have to fall in on its own, but yes, that's essentially it, ma'am."

Jacinta felt herself scowling. The whole idea was preposterous, but what else did they have?

"Will this work?" Jacinta asked Hially.

The alien captain in the little girl's body gave a slight shrug. "I suppose it's not impossible."

Jacinta almost groaned. "Get started."

Jameson grinned and headed down to the floor where he opened a heavily guarded crate which housed all the equipment they'd recovered from the awakened prior to this mission. Before they'd been assigned here, Mike had insisted it be stored onsite in case of an emergency, and right now she could have kissed him for it.

CHAPTER 24

A deep tearing sound issued from somewhere outside the building, similar to thunder, but less natural. Jacinta couldn't help but compulsively look out through the destroyed section of the factory wall to see what was happening.

Jameson and two of his men had returned to the machine and were excavating the concrete below in order to attempt their mad plan. From the looks of what was occurring outside, they wouldn't have long to make it work.

The mass was splitting into segments from its top, not unlike a banana peel being removed on a giant scale. As the sections split away, thousands, perhaps tens of thousands of cells began raining from its surface. A crystalline clinking was audible even from here as they shattered on the ground.

"Here we go," Jacinta muttered as the first rumble of jet engines reached her ears.

"No," Hially said from beside her. "Those are the inert cells of the outer layer. It's what comes next you need to fear."

With a crash that sent vibrations all the way to their hiding spot, the four sections of the mass' exterior fell away to reveal a translucent greenish core. The mass pulsated. Once, twice, then began shedding what was apparently a thin outer layer, sloughing it off as though it were discarding an unwanted jacket.

A pair of fighter planes zipped overhead, their jet engines roaring as they began a first probing attack run. Jacinta held her breath, and even Hially seemed curious as to the result.

"Come on," Jacinta urged under her breath.

The fighters raced towards the mass, taking only seconds to close the few remaining kilometres to the target.

One of the planes veered away, rolling and banking in a wild manoeuvre as it sought to avoid some response from the mass. The second plane stayed on course and dropped its payload a second later before veering off to join its wingman. Both of the pilots began a slow loop to take them back towards the target.

The bomb hit the mass square on, but instead of the bright explosion Jacinta expected, the payload seemed to spread a white-hot substance onto the mass. The entire structure quivered and receded where the weapon made contact.

"What was that?" Hially asked, genuinely curious.

"Thermite," Lindel replied. "If your information was correct, it should be effective. Unfortunately, we only have a limited number of weapons we can equip with the substance at short notice. They won't be enough on their own."

In the distance, the mass began pulsating again, sloughing off another layer of itself onto the ground. Jacinta expected it to land on top of the first, but was horrified to see that the previously ejected layer was now beyond the range of the new cells. The substance was already moving out in every direction, and given its speed, it couldn't be more than an hour from the nearest part of the harbour.

"Jameson, it's spreading. You need to hurry."

"Yes, ma'am," Jameson responded without looking up. "Just a few more minutes."

Above the mass, the pair of fighter jets were heading back to the mass in a hurry. They were almost there when the first plane simply exploded, the blast clipping his wingman and sending the aircraft spiralling down into the mass itself. Just before it hit, Jacinta swore she saw the thermite weapon detach. Then it and the plane were gone, leaving the mass quivering, but outwardly unaffected in its wake. She strained to see, but from here, no chute was visible.

"How many of those weapons do we have?" Jacinta asked Lindel as they waited tensely for Jameson and his men to finish their work.

"One moment," Lindel replied as she got back on the communications link to Rush Base.

"Ninety-eight remaining," she announced a moment later.

"Tell them to hold fire until we've activated the weapon. We'll need every last one to control the spread of any cells that survive."

Lindel nodded, then began conversing with someone at the base again, probably Jeff.

"Alright, everyone stand back. This isn't exactly by the book," Jameson called out.

The newly excavated ditch under the front half of the machine extended almost to its midline, and was about ten feet deep at the leading edge. Those makeshift weapons the awakened had constructed were impressive, she had to admit. At least when not being used against her own men. Even now, she was still having trouble shaking the nightmares about the carnage she'd witnessed when she'd first entered Victoria's safe house.

She shook off the unproductive line of thought as Jameson got down on the ground. He used the weapon to melt away the final piece of flooring, sending the giant machine past the tipping point and allowing it to slide into the ditch they'd prepared.

Without warning, it slowly tilted towards a precarious forty-five-degree angle before thudding down the short incline. With a thundering ring of metal on concrete, the construction screeched to a halt.

"Is it enough?" Jacinta demanded as soon as the grinding ceased.

"Checking," Hially said, already working on a computer she'd rigged as a temporary interface.

"Attempting target lock now," the young girl said.

The machine creaked as she fed it instructions, the aperture moving spasmodically as it did its best to comply with her instructions.

Outside, the mass was pulsating again, sloughing off a third layer of cells. This was taking too long. There must be thousands of them out there now, heading in every direction. The first layer had nearly reached the edge of the impact zone. Once they got into the cover of the surrounding buildings, they would be much harder to target and destroy.

The machine creaked and protested as it moved, but eventually ground into its programmed position.

"That's it," Hially called.

"Fire in thirty seconds," Jacinta responded. "Lindel inform the General that any troops in the area should take cover. Everyone else, move away from the machine."

The analyst was already on the comms before Jacinta finished speaking. The rest of the support staff were heading for the back of the building as fast as they could go.

A moment later Lindel nodded that it was done, and they all watched as the next layer of cells finished sloughing off the mass and began to move away.

"Firing in ten seconds," Hially announced to the silent room. "Five, four, three…"

The machine hummed, a deep green glow forming around the aperture. A lance of light struck out, stunningly strong, and made contact with the target. The shot burnt a hole right through its heart and shattered a skyscraper which happened to be in its line of fire several kilometres behind.

8:17

"No!" Jacinta gasped as the beam faded and the immense building tumbled, silent at this distance. "What did you do!"

"What you asked," Hially answered, seeming somewhat confused.

"You destroyed a building! Do you know how many people you just killed?"

Hially sighed. "You still don't understand. Anyone not already evacuated at that range is already dead. They cannot outrun the mass at that distance, and with this many cells on the ground, their numbers will never thin out. They will reproduce as they go, and their increase will be such that the circle of cells will grow ever wider as it expands outward.

"But we just…"

"Yes, we've done a lot of damage to the mass. That blast will have killed a hundred thousand cells or more. Unfortunately it has also allowed the remaining cells a way out without the mass having to slough them off. Every remaining cell will be free to escape at once."

Jacinta looked out the ruined factory wall and felt her heart drop. The hole the machine had left was a gaping wound in the pulsating mass. At least two thirds of it had been vaporised, but what remained was collapsing into a viscous puddle that writhed of its own accord, several metres deep.

"Tell the General to bring everything he has to bear on that mass right now," Jacinta ordered. "If it makes it to the ocean…"

Lindel wasted no time acknowledging the order, and within seconds of her conversing over the comms, the sound of jet engines once again became audible overhead.

"The General wants to know if we can fire again?" she asked after a moment.

Hially shook her head. "Unfortunately not. These weapons were designed for a single shot before draining the power supply. There's nothing more we can do here."

Lindel nodded without showing any particular emotion, and relayed the information back to the base. Jacinta hoped she looked half as calm at the news.

"Acknowledged," Lindel said before taking off the headset she'd been wearing since the outset.

"We're ordered to evacuate the support staff by land, the General is sending a helicopter for key personnel. He wants us back at the base asap to help coordinate and advise."

8:17

Jacinta turned to the main part of the room before raising her voice.

"Listen up! All military, awakened, and A.T.U. personnel are to fall back to Rush Base via vehicle on the double. Grab your weapons and gear and move out."

"Jameson, issue whatever remains of the awakened's captured weapons to the soldiers in the convoy, just in case."

"Yes ma'am," he said straight faced.

Jacinta felt her lips purse in irritation, then scowled as he turned away with a slight grin she was sure he hadn't meant her to see.

For a long moment the room was filled with activity, and she took the time to walk over to the gaping hole in the factory wall.

The sight before her was grim.

What appeared to be two full squadrons of fighter jets, both F/A-18F's and the new F-35 Lightning II's were expending their ammunition at a frightening rate. They seemed to be working on two fronts. The first flight was intent on eliminating as much of the remaining central mass as possible, while the other squadron was circling the area, attempting to burn a perimeter around the expanding ring of cells.

The mass had expanded outward more quickly than she would have believed, and was already halfway between the crash site and where they were hiding. She had to believe that it had made it a similar distance in every direction. The cells were like an undulating carpet across every surface they'd expanded to. She did a quick bit of math. If the radius of the mass had expanded to a kilometre, that meant a perimeter of over three kilometres. All of which needed to be bombed just to stop them expanding further.

How many thermite bombs did it take to burn a three-kilometre circle in the ground at over three thousand degrees, then fill in that entire area? More than they had on hand, certainly.

It wasn't going to work.

In the distance she could see army trucks approaching in a massive convoy, and wondered what they planned to do. Flamethrowers might be effective in at least slowing the enemy down she supposed.

As the factory emptied around her, Jacinta watched as the convoy began setting entire streets worth of houses and factories on fire ahead of the alien advance. It wouldn't be as hot as the airborne weapon drops, but every bit that slowed the enemy advance was useful.

8:17

Above, the fighter jets were already heading out of the area to rearm and refuel. Until they returned, the ground forces were all that stood between the creatures and the ocean. Even now, only the northern edge of the perimeter, closest to the water and CBD, was truly aflame. To the west, the main army convoy was continuing to burn its defensive line. At the rate the cells were moving, it wouldn't be long until those defences were tested. To the east and south, there was nothing. The jets would likely attack the eastern advance next as it moved towards the harbour. To the south, where the factory was located, there was precious little to stop any cells which might have outpaced the pack.

"Can you detonate this machine?" she blurted out as the idea hit her.

Hially nodded slowly from further back in the building.

"Yes, the machines all had a tamper proof failsafe installed. I believe you saw the results firsthand," she nodded towards Lindel.

The analyst's mouth tightened, her hands balling into fists, but she just nodded.

"You know it won't stop the advance."

"No," Jacinta responded. "But it might buy us a bit more time. At the very least there will be that many fewer cells which can reproduce."

Hially nodded. "If that is your wish."

"E.T.A. on our chopper?" Jacinta asked as she headed back to the others.

"Three minutes, twenty seconds," Lindel responded without needing to check again.

"Set it for four and a half minutes."

"No need," Hially said. "I can detonate it remotely once we're out of the blast range."

Jacinta stopped for a moment, unsure what to say. The A.T.U. had known about the failsafe, but that Hially's people could detonate the machines at will was horrifying.

She shook her head to clear it.

"Very well. If there's nothing more we can do here we should get outside to the evac point. Take whatever you need and let's go. Jameson, lead the way."

"Yes ma'am," the man responded with a grin.

They traversed the short distance without incident, Jameson leading with the awakened's weapon held in front like a blocky pistol. Lindel had her computer, and Hially the laptop on which she had rigged up her interface. The rest of the support staff were gone, their cars just driving out of sight around a distant corner as Jacinta exited the building behind the others. To her right, she could see down a shallow decline to where the mass of creatures were squirming forward, metre by metre, covering every surface as they passed. She tried to look behind them, to see what was left in their wake, but even now the central mass was still sending out more cells. The mass now blanketed everything in a kilometre wide radius like a viscous and mostly translucent moving carpet.

"This is very bad," Hially said as the group stopped to stare at the horrendous sight. "With this many cells still active it is equivalent to starting my projection on day four. I'm sorry, my ships will not arrive here in time. If you have any vessels capable of orbital or sustained high atmospheric flight, I advise you to launch them before it's too late."

Jacinta felt her mouth open and close, but no words came to mind. Hially's shoulders had slumped, and the look in her eyes conveyed a weariness that no child of her age could ever have known.

"You're a stubborn people, but a brave one. When my fleet arrives, we'll gladly take on board any survivors."

The sound of a chopper coming in for a landing drowned out any need for a response. The four of them turned their backs to the aircraft as it kicked up clouds of dust and debris from the abandoned carpark as it landed.

As they piled in, the crew of the old Blackhawk handed them headsets so they could hear and speak to each other over the noise of the aircraft. A few seconds later they were lifting off again, and Jacinta secured herself to the seat as the helicopter banked upward.

"Captain, take us over the battle line and hold position."

"Negative Agent Robbins, my orders are to return you and your people to Rush Base."

"Captain, the only reason they want me back at command is to advise them on what we've seen firsthand. I can't do that if I haven't seen what is about to happen here firsthand, now can I?"

"I'm sorry ma'am, my orders come from the General himself. Your people are priority evacuees."

"Wait a minute, you're part of the evacuation effort?" Jameson interrupted over the headset.

"Obviously," The captain responded.

"Under General Blake's command?"

"Yes sir," the pilot responded.

"Captain," Jacinta took over again after a thankful nod to Jameson. "You do know that General Blake has been relieved of duty?"

8:17

There was a long moment of silence as the pilot and co-pilot shared a look.

"Ma'am, it is my understanding that General Blake is still in charge of the evacuation."

"That's true. The General's experience is being utilised in that capacity, however he is no longer in command of this mission. If you need confirmation, contact General Huon or A.T.U. Director Illum at joint command."

Again there was a long stretch of silence, long enough that Jacinta wondered if the pilot was confirming his orders, or ignoring her completely.

At ground level, the rough circle of the mass was about to make contact with the defensive line the army had set up. She had to know how effective the line of soldiers was if she were to advise on further defence.

"Orders confirmed," A voice broke into her headset. "We're to place ourselves at your disposal Agent Robbins. Heading back to the front now."

The helicopter banked again as the pilot changed course, bringing them around so they could monitor the situation from above.

"Can you patch us into their communications?" she asked the pilot.

"One moment," the response came back.

Despite their somewhat rocky start, the man was clearly competent.

"Remember, hold the line, nothing gets through. There is no backup coming if we fall. Fire."

The voice on the comms was deep and scratchy. The kind of voice that had spent a career yelling at fresh recruits. Jacinta craned her neck to see out the door as they approached.

A dozen flamethrowers burst into life as the mass approached the wall of burning buildings. It seemed the commander down there wanted to keep the barrier burning hot rather than attacking the mass directly. At the rate the cells were spreading, it might even work. The helicopter moved into position and hovered. Jacinta stood, moving to the window where she took firm hold of the doorframe and leaned out.

They were several hundred feet off the ground, and the cars looked like toys, while the surrounding streets appeared something off a children's playmat. At least until you encountered the mass. The translucent carpet continued pushing forward despite the cells at the front appearing to retract at the heat of the blaze.

Like a wave approaching the shore, a second layer of the mass rolled over the first. Another viscous layer that again attempted to retract as it came in contact with the inferno. A third layer pushed forward, clearly being hurt, but having no choice but to keep moving. The layer behind it continued to pulse forward, pushing it into range of the flames as well. Again and again a row of cells would slough over the top, propelled by those behind it, unable to stop as they began to burn. Yet even with all its casualties, the mass gained ground with each wave. Within a minute the cells reached the outer edge of the houses themselves and were still being shoved forward. In instants, the never-ending mass was putting out the fires, smothering the outskirts of the immolated barricade with the weight of their own dead bodies.

"They're at the factory," Hially announced.

"Blow it," Jacinta ordered, and the young girl, or at least the alien inhabiting her body, pressed the screen in front of her without hesitation.

A moment passed, then a there was a deep boom. The whole factory disappeared in an implosion which sucked in everything in a hundred metre radius. The ground fell away and collapsed, and every cell nearby was vaporised in the blast. For a moment the helicopter rocked violently before the pilot got it back under control.

The aircraft steadied off as a huge plume of dust

rose from the mangled site where the weapon had been located. The blast must have killed thousands of cells, but the ones behind them didn't even hesitate. They simply slid forward down the depression left by the blast as if nothing untoward had happened.

Jacinta couldn't quite believe what she was seeing, the mass had no concern for its losses at all.

She turned back to look at the battle raging below. At either end of the defensive line, the cells were continuing their outward spread unimpeded, and the soldiers were shifting to defence as their flanks became more and more exposed.

"They need to get out of there before they're cut off," Jameson said from behind.

The sound of the jets returning was audible even above the noise of the helicopter. Jacinta looked out the other side of the aircraft to see the squadrons laying down thermite explosives on the eastern side of the mass, attempting to block their access to the harbour.

That was entirely out of her control, and Jacinta turned back to the fight below her, which was becoming desperate.

Row after row of cells was being expended to douse the flames in front of them, but it didn't seem to matter. There were hundreds more rows behind them, all pushing the others forward. She doubted the men on the ground had enough ordinance to deal with them all.

The cells everywhere except the defensive line continued to ignore it, moving outward on a mission of their own. Below, artillery pieces, and shoulder mounted rocket launchers were firing into the mass. They caused damage for a moment, but whatever holes they created in the enemy lines were filled in an instant as if the weapons had never been used.

It didn't stop the men below firing off more ordinance than anyone in this country had ever seen. It was hard to tell just how many soldiers were down there, but it had to be at least a thousand.

Tracer rounds flew from rifles in place of bullets, causing the creatures to flinch, but little more than that. Those few who were halted were simply rolled over by the next cell behind, and all the while the mass churned forward.

Less than a minute after contact, the defensive line of buildings had been doused by the slowly melting bodies of cells pushed forward by those behind. The line of soldiers with their flamethrowers were now having to attack the mass itself. For a minute more they held it back, the hotter, direct flames of their weapons seeming to have more of an effect.

Then the first flamethrower ran out of fuel.

To say the mass surged forward was inaccurate. It was more that it was no longer being held back. Cell after viscous cell sloughed over the bodies of their burnt companions as the soldiers desperately tried to refuel the weapon in time.

Just as they seemed to be ready, another unit next to them ran out

Along the line, three more units reached their operational limit and went quiet. The wave of creatures humped towards the men now desperately firing everything they had left at the mass.

It wasn't enough. Even from this height Jacinta could hear the screams of men as the mass simply rolled over them. It didn't even speed up as it melted and absorbed their flesh into itself; the action bereft of all anger or malice.

It was only then that Jacinta understood what Hially had been telling her. This wasn't the attack of an enemy, this was an instinctually driven creature feeding and surviving in the only way it knew how. There would be no negotiating, no ceasefire, no chance of reprieve. This wasn't a war. The mass was a predator, and everything was its prey.

"We've got to do something!" Jameson yelled through the headset.

8:17

Jacinta wanted to say something, to suggest some possible plan, but in the end all she could do was shrug.

"I'm open to suggestions."

Jameson just looked at her pleadingly. The man had been military before joining the A.T.U. There was every chance he knew some of those men even now being overrun by the implacable mass below.

"Captain, fire whatever ordinance you're carrying in defence of those men."

"Acknowledged."

The chopper tilted forward and a series of missiles left smoke trails as the pilots obeyed her order. If the explosives had any effect, the damaged cells were replaced within moments to the point that she couldn't even see where the weapons had hit.

Her top soldier's mouth opened and closed without sound as the chopper levelled off, then his shoulders slumped as he turned back to the open doorway.

There was nothing they could do from here and he knew it. The mass was just too large, and it was still spreading, now covering what must be close to a two-kilometre radius from the crash site. Everywhere except in front of the shrinking line of defenders, it hadn't even paused. Even the area where the jet fighters had dropped their first round of ordinance seemed to have cooled enough that the mass was once again pushing up against it. If it behaved the same way it had here, it would penetrate that flaming barrier in moments. At the rate it was moving, it would reach the ocean in only another twenty minutes.

A few of the last remaining men below had scrambled up onto a three-storey rooftop and were continuing to burn the mass with one of the last operational flamethrowers. It was a brave stand, but about as effective as spraying an anthill with a small water pistol.

"We have to get them out of there!" Jameson yelled over the headsets.

"Negative sir, there isn't time," the pilot's dispassionate voice came back.

The mass kept coming, in seconds piling up burnt cells near the building's wall until the wave simply rolled over the rooftop and the men making their futile last stand.

"Take us back to Rush Base, Captain," Jacinta felt sick as she said it.

"Yes ma'am," came the tightly controlled response.

Jameson pounded the doorframe as the chopper

turned away from the scene of the slaughter. There was nothing to be gained by staying. No one remained to be saved. The mass moved on, caring nothing for the 'battle' it had just fought, nor the lives it had extinguished. Around where those brave men had died, the leading edge of the mass had arced inward, spreading to meet itself again in a seamless wall. The section delayed by the battle humped forward to fill the gap, rapidly catching up with the rest now that they were no longer being slowed down.

Jacinta felt sick. The whole affair had taken less than five minutes, and as the helicopter banked back towards the base, it was impossible to even tell where it had taken place. A thousand men, with all the munitions they could carry, hadn't halted the expanding front for an instant.

"I'm sorry. I tried to warn you that your technology wasn't a match for the enemy," Hially said over the headset.

"Captain, put me through to General Huon and Director Illum," Lindel said grimly.

Jacinta had seen the woman scared, confused, awed, and challenged over the last several months working on this case. The tone in her voice now sent shivers up Jacinta's spine.

"What is it?" she asked the analyst.

Lindel ignored her completely. Staring out the door at the vast alien mass below.

"Huon here, report," came over the comms a few moments later.

"Is Director Illum there as well," she asked.

"I'm here," Jeff confirmed.

"Good. General, Director, the mass is undeterred and moving at approximately six kilometres per hour. All assets lost. Mission ineffective. Repeat, mission ineffective. Recommend immediate deployment of Project Emu. Say again, recommend immediate deployment of Project Emu. Failure threshold, eighteen minutes."

There was a silence over the comm link as the command staff digested that bit of news, but General Huon responded with a curt, 'understood' before cutting the link.

Everyone in the chopper was silent after the exchange, but Jacinta was left with one burning question.

"What is Project Emu? What did you just do?"

Lindel looked at her for a moment before slightly shaking her head.

"I'm sorry, it's classified."

"I'm second in charge of the A.T.U. I have top level clearance," Jacinta responded. She was not in a mood have her questions evaded.

"That you know about." Lindel told her. "There are… certain projects, which exceed the normal security precautions. Their existence is known only to the Prime Minister, a few top generals, and the staff required for their inception."

"And you were part of that inception, for this Project Emu, I take it?"

Lindel nodded defiantly.

"Until today, I have always regretted my part in making it a reality. After seeing what just happened to those men though, I don't think I do anymore."

Jacinta thought furiously. What kind of weapon could Lindel have possibly designed that could make a dent in that?

She looked out the door again, past Jameson and down to the seething mass below.

It was almost at the limits of the city centre now. Beyond the rows of high-rise buildings lay the iconic harbour bridge, and the deep water it straddled. There was nothing else left in between.

CHAPTER 25

Six minutes later they were touching down at Rush Base, the helicopter swirling dust as it approached the pad.

"Let's go!" Jacinta yelled over the whine of the rotors. Jameson jumped out and helped Hially to the ground. Lindel and Jacinta followed closely behind.

As soon as they were clear, the aircraft took off again and a man in uniform came to meet them from a nearby doorway.

"Agent Robbins, come with me please. I'm to escort you and your people to the situation room."

Jacinta nodded and motioned him to lead the way. It was the same officer who had all but kidnapped her from her home when Victoria had agreed to talk. Such things were of little consequence at this point.

He led the way into the nearby building, which was little more than the entrance to an elevator shaft. He inserted his key card, and a button labelled 'SB3' began to flash.

As he pressed the button, the doors closed, and the lift lurched into a rapid descent. How far they went underground she couldn't be certain, but it sure wasn't a normal set of building floors.

Half a minute later they slowed just as rapidly, and the doors opened on to a bland corridor of concrete and metal. The construction was sturdy, but without even so much as a coat of paint other than several coloured lines which ran down the middle of the floor. They would no doubt lead you to various areas of the base, if you knew what the colours represented.

The officer led them through a series of corridors at a fast pace. Even so, Lindel seemed to want to rush ahead. Soon enough they came to a door guarded by a pair of soldiers with advanced body armour and automatic rifles.

The officer didn't even give them a second glance as he opened the door with his key card and led them inside.

As the doors opened, they revealed a room full of screens and readouts. The technicians behind every desk were in a state of something close to panic. It reminded her of nothing more that the scenes in movies where NASA's mission control was attempting to avert some global level disaster.

Probably not too far from the truth, she thought as a barrel-chested man stood from where he was leaning over a screen near the front of the room.

"Good, you're here," he said without preamble.

"Is Project Emu ready to be deployed?" Lindel broke in as if she commanded the room.

"Almost," General Huon replied. "It's being armed as we speak."

"You need to hurry General; we have little time."

"Thank you Miss Harding, I'm well aware of the situation," the huge man said as he approached their group.

"No sir, with all respect, you're not. Those men you sent out there, they weren't defeated in battle by a superior force. The mass didn't care about them at all, didn't fight with them, they were simply in its way. It consumed them because they were a natural fuel source along its path, and while they were occupied, every other cell kept moving. If the mass extends beyond the limits of Project Emu's range, we will not be able to stop it. If that occurs, the entire world will suffer the same fate as those men. We have eight minutes left to deploy the weapon. If we fail, nothing else in our arsenal, or anyone else's, will get the job done in time."

"I understand the situation," Huon repeated through clenched teeth. "Those were my men out there, Miss Harding, some of whom I served with for many years… And you," he said, abruptly changing tack.

"You must be Captain Hially."

The body of the young girl nodded sagely, unaffected by the General's mood, or his imposing size.

"Perhaps you could explain to me why every single one of those weapons around the globe you built to supposedly protect us just melted down?"

Jacinta just looked at Hially in shock. She'd assumed it was only the weapon they'd been stationed at which had self-destructed.

"They were no longer relevant."

"No longer relevant?" The General almost choked. "The most powerful weapons systems' on this planet, were no longer relevant. In the middle of an invasion…"

"That's correct General. They were makeshift inventions, and useless against a ground assault. Once my fleet arrives, we will set up more permanent defences to safeguard this star system, and if you somehow survive, this world in particular."

"We'll survive," Huon said with a scowl.

"Excuse me, General, but what exactly is this 'Project Emu', and why give something so deadly such a ridiculous name?" Jacinta interrupted.

Huon just gave her a flat look.

"Tell her," he said to Lindel before turning away, striding over to confer with one of the busy technicians at a nearby desk.

Lindel frowned and looked at the floor as the General left.

"What do you know about 'The Great Emu War?'"

"The what?" Jacinta asked, almost laughing out loud at the absurdity of the question.

Lindel sighed. "In nineteen thirty-two, approximately twenty thousand emus migrated to an area outside Perth. The region's economic recovery after the great depression was slow, and the birds were causing a huge problem to local farmers and their crops. Someone decided it would be a good idea to send in soldiers with old machine guns from World War One to eliminate the animals, which had been declared vermin."

8:17

"You're kidding?"

Lindel just shook her head. "It gets worse. Those soldiers attempted to take on a group of nearly a thousand emus and succeeded in killing some, but the rest just scattered throughout the region. With those old-style weapons it was taking about ten bullets to kill each of the birds, even when the men could get them in range. This result was repeated several times until after about a month of expensive and ineffective attempts, the government declared a halt to the extermination program."

"Wait. The emu's won?"

"The emu's won," Lindel confirmed. "Despite the soldiers' massive advantages in both technology and intelligence, the Emu numbers were so great that they couldn't be defeated with the resources at hand."

"Hence, Project Emu," Jacinta confirmed.

Lindel nodded. "Australia is a small country in every way except physical size. There are cities in the world with larger populations than our entire nation. Project Emu was designed as a failsafe so that an invading army couldn't simply overwhelm us with numbers in a surprise attack."

"Okay, but what is it?" Jacinta asked again.

Lindel took a deep breath before looking her in the eyes. "Project Emu is a thirty-kiloton nuclear warhead capable of being mounted on a ballistic missile."

"What?!" Jacinta gasped.

General Huon looked up with a slight grin from where he'd been listening in on their conversation.

"We're the second largest supplier of uranium in the world, Agent Robbins. Did you really think we didn't know how to use it?"

"That's what you want to use on Sydney?"

Lindel's expression became offended.

"Of course I don't want to use it, but you've seen what we're facing, what the world is facing. Do you have another option? Anything at all? Anything that will mean we don't have to murder at least a million of our own people with a weapon I helped our government illegally construct…"

Jacinta could only open and close her mouth in silence.

"Sir," a nearby technician announced. "I have confirmation that Project Emu is armed and ready for deployment.

Huon nodded. "Good. With three minutes to spare. Remove final fail safes, prepare to launch."

8:17

"Major Smith, insert your arming key and turn on my signal."

A nearby officer nodded curtly after an instant's hesitation, and removed a small silver key from a chain hidden around his neck, beneath his uniform.

"Sergeant Jasper, reroute our fighter planes to their base outside the city, then get me the Prime Minister on the screen."

"Aye Sir," an officer at the next desk responded.

The General moved to the panel Major Smith was now standing at and took out another key from around his own neck. He took a deep breath and inserted it into its slot.

"Turn on my mark," he said.

Smith nodded.

"Three, two, one, turn," Huon counted in steady rhythm. As he spoke the final word, both men turned their key to the right, and the panel came alive with readouts. A conspicuous red button under a clear glass cover began to flash.

"Set target coordinates to the alien crash site," Huon ordered.

Smith nodded and began working on one of the console displays.

Without warning, half the gigantic screen at the front of the room switched to a view of the cabinet meeting room in Canberra. The various ministers and Prime Minister sat at a large wooden table with expressions ranging from severe to teary.

"Coordinates set and locked," Smith announced.

Huon nodded.

"Prime Minister, Ministers. Project Emu is armed and ready to deploy on your order. Request permission to remove cover and access fire control."

The Prime Minister nodded gravely.

General Huon hesitated.

"I'm going to need you to say the words, Sir. For the record."

The Prime Minister swallowed hard, but nodded again. "Remove the cover, access Project Emu's firing control General Huon."

"Yes Sir," the General confirmed. He spent a moment inputting a code into a keypad below the glass case, and there was a slight click. He pulled the case upward, and when it separated from the panel, he handed it to Major Smith.

"Ready to fire," he said gravely to the men and women on the screen.

8:17

Jacinta could only stare in horror at what was happening. Every bone in her body was screaming at her to stop what was about to happen, but what else could they do? On the other half of the screen, the satellite feed was showing the mass expanding outward all too rapidly. It wasn't going to stop. There wasn't going to be some unexpected reprieve at the last minute. This was going to happen.

There was a crash behind her and several armed soldiers came rushing in to take up positions around the room. Behind them, General Blake strode in.

"Stand down!" he ordered the entire room. "Everybody in this area is hereby charged with treason. You will go with these men to a holding area until such time as you can prosecuted for your crimes."

CHAPTER 26

"General Blake, what is the meaning of this!" The Prime Ministers voice boomed over the screen. "General Huon is following the orders of this cabinet."

"Oh, I know he's following your orders," Huon replied. "Don't worry, I have men on the way to take you into custody as well."

"We don't have time for this, Blake. You have already been relieved of rank prior to this action, and have no lawful authority to do anything you're suggesting."

"You mean like you had no lawful authority to develop a nuclear weapon against every treaty this country has ever signed?"

There was some nervous shuffling amongst the cabinet members at that, but the Prime Minister stood, leaning forward with his hands pressed firmly against the table.

8:17

"Look at the screen, Blake. I know you can see what's happening out there right now. Just as we can. Tell me you have another option we can implement in the next two minutes, and we'll listen..."

Blake snarled at the screen. "You know I don't. But that doesn't mean I'm going to let you nuke our own people. Large forces from both the U.S. and China are already on their way here, I'm confident that between them we can overcome this... infection."

"With all due respect General Blake," Hially interrupted. "By the time they arrive, the mass will have entered the ocean. Your weapons will be ineffective once that occurs. This is the only way."

"And we're to take her word for that?" Blake demanded of the leaders on the screen. "An eight-year-old girl who has spent the better part of the last year in a coma? That's what we're basing murdering a million of our people on?"

"No General, we are basing it on the word of an alien commander who has so far demonstrated knowledge and technology which could not possibly have originated on this planet. We are basing it on what we can see with our own eyes and verify with our own equipment. We are basing on the fact that a thousand of our soldiers were just slaughtered for no effect against the enemy at all. And we are basing it on the fact that as much as it galls us, there is more than just our nation and our citizens at stake. General Huon, fire the weapon. That is a direct order."

"Yes Sir," Huon said from where he was still standing near the firing console. That an armed serviceman was pointing a rifle at his back didn't seem to concern the huge man at all.

"I won't let you do it," Blake told his replacement flatly.

"What would you have us do Blake?" Huon asked, frustration getting the better of him. "Go down swinging in a blaze of glory until every one of us is dead?"

"Better that than turning on our own people."

Huon harrumphed. "So it's somehow better in your mind for all of us to die, than just some of us? You're a military man, well versed in both tactics and leadership. Tell me, how is that a victory?"

"One minute until launch window closes!" a technician called, silencing the argument.

"Enough of this," The Prime Minister demanded. "Fire the weapon."

"If he moves, shoot him," Blake ordered the soldier still standing behind Huon.

"This is your Prime Minister giving a direct order

to all loyal personnel remaining in the command centre. Take that room back by force and launch the weapon by any means necessary. We are out of time!"

Jacinta shared a meaningful look with Lindel and motioned the analyst to make herself scarce. Lindel nodded and subtly moved Hially behind her.

General Huon lunged at the firing control, and in what seemed a reflex reaction, the man behind him fired four bullets into his back. As the huge General crumpled to the floor, the soldier stood there, wide eyed as if even he couldn't believe what had just happened.

"Get down!" Jacinta yelled to Lindel and Hially.

In response to the General's death, men and women across the room began launching themselves at the handful of armed soldiers who had invaded the command centre.

Jameson all but tackled her behind a desk, pulling Lindel and Hially into the dubious cover as well a moment later.

"Stay down," Jameson hissed as he peeked around the desk momentarily before rushing out to join the fray.

"We have to fire that weapon!" Lindel said to

Jacinta, who nodded curtly, the analyst still flinching every time a gun went off.

"Stay hidden," Jacinta told Hially.

Peeking out as Jameson had a moment before, she saw the unarmed agent wrestling with General Blake on the floor, both men attempting to get hold of his sidearm. Most of the other guards had been rushed by the command room personnel, but one was free and firing into the crowd.

Jacinta pointed to the right of the desk meaningfully and Lindel nodded.

Taking a deep breath, Jacinta stood, raising her hands and making the unoccupied soldier focus in her direction.

"Don't fire, I'm unarmed," she said, circling to the left.

"On your knees!" the man yelled. "Now!"

"Okay," Jacinta replied in her most calming tone.

"I'm doing as you say, don't shoot."

From the corner of her eye she could see Lindel had crawled away from their hiding place. Though unfortunately Hially seemed to have gone with her.

A shot rang out and the man pointing a gun at her clutched at his chest before falling to the floor, injured but alive. The technician who had shot him turned his weapon towards the General, but he was too slow, and fell silently as a hole appeared in his head. General Blake was slowly getting to his feet, the pistol outstretched.

Where was Jameson?

Jacinta got to her feet and let her arms fall, gaining the man's attention.

"Enough!" Blake roared, though with all his other soldiers engaged in hand-to-hand combat, this time no one listened.

From here she could see Jameson lying prone on the floor, a deep cut on his forehead where the General appeared to have struck him with his pistol butt.

Jacinta slowly moved further into the room. She didn't need to reach the button herself, only to give Lindel enough time to do so.

"General, please, you've seen what's happening out there. This has to end."

She continued moving into the room until she was blocking the man's line of sight to the firing button. She wasn't large though, and it would only be a fraction of the console she was hiding.

"I can't let you do it!" Blake yelled again.

"But why?" Jacinta demanded. "It's the only possible path to the survival of the human race. Why are you trying to stop us?"

"Because my children are in the blast zone!" Blake's voice almost broke, and Jacinta knew it was the truth.

Her shoulders slumped. Any hope she'd harboured of reasoning with the man gone at those words.

"I'm sorry. Truly. But are you really willing to sacrifice the entire human race so they can live a few minutes longer? You have to realise that if they are close enough to be in range of the blast, they are too close to escape the mass even if we don't fire."

"You don't know that, and I won't let you kill them."

"Weapon launched," a computerised voice declared.

"No!" Blake screamed. Jacinta dived away, but not before his first shot took her in the arm.

She screamed as her wounded arm hit the floor. From down here she could see that Hially had crawled under the console while she'd been talking with Blake. The girl was lying prone, one arm still reaching upwards around its leading edge, her hand still on the button.

"What have you done!" Blake screamed at the alien

captain/young girl staring at him from underneath the console.

"Saved your world," she said as the General reoriented his weapon.

Face contorted with fury and despair, the General's legs flew out from beneath him as Jameson kicked him hard in the back of the knees. The soldier was still down himself, and as the big man tumbled backwards, Jameson applied a swift elbow to his head as the General hit the floor. The double impact was enough to knock Blake out, and Jameson nodded to her slightly, still woozy from his own injury.

Around the room, all the fight had gone out of the soldiers trying to disrupt the operation as soon as the weapon had been launched. In fact, with Blake now down, the entire room was still, silent, and focused on the large screen at the front of the room.

"Twenty seconds until impact," a lone voice called from a station near the corner.

On the screen, the mass had reached the city centre now. Far from slowing down though, the cells were crawling up skyscrapers and humping along narrow streets where their numbers forced them into piles dozens of metres high. It didn't deter them at all.

The worst part though were the people. Thousands of them were streaming from the buildings in a futile attempt to get away from the mass. They weren't fast enough, and it just rolled over them, absorbing their flesh as it went.

Jacinta abruptly found herself grateful the image didn't come with sound.

"Ten seconds till impact," the technician called.

"Are we safe down here?" Jameson asked quietly as he made his way back to her.

Jacinta clasped her injured arm a little tighter.

"After what we just helped to do, I'm not even sure I care," she responded, eyes still glued to the screen.

He didn't respond to that, instead, choosing to invest his attention on what was about to occur.

There was a flash of movement on the screen and then a blinding white light before the video feed cut out. A moment later the entire room began to shake. Fluorescent lightbulbs shattered in their brackets, chairs skittered across the floor like unbalanced washing machines, and cracks appeared in the poured concrete walls. An instant later, every piece of equipment in the room sparked and died, leaving them in the pitch-black confines of a chamber several hundred metres below the surface. The structure continued to shake and crack around them.

CHAPTER 27

Hours had passed since the blast, or at least it felt that way in the darkness. A few flashlights had been recovered from somewhere, but those were being used by the technicians attempting to restore power to the command bunker.

General Blake and his men had been arrested and confined to a cell without further resistance. A medic had staunched her wound and bandaged it as best he could in the dim light. The bullet had gone right through, and despite the extraordinary amount of pain she was in, the medic assured her she would be alright.

Of course, that was a relative term. A nuclear blast had gone off not ten kilometres from where they stood. Although the solid rock between had shielded them from the blast, and was now keeping out the radiation, there was every chance they were going to be trapped down here for a good long while. All of which assumed that the bomb had done its job. If it hadn't, the mass would have long since reached the sea, dooming the rest of humanity to a swift and violent end.

There were raised voices from the other end of the room before she abruptly heard Director Illum settle the matter in no uncertain terms.

Jeff had been down at the front of the room when she'd arrived, and preoccupied with other matters. Once Blake had burst in, the director had been the one to take down the first of the soldiers the General had brought with him. It had been enough to break the others free from their shock and join the brawl, which had cost eight of the command staff their lives.

Although the imminent danger had passed, tensions remained elevated, and would until they knew what had happened up on the surface.

Lindel and a technician were hip deep in the wiring of a console near the front of the room. The analyst was attempting to rewire the base's communications system so they could at least find out whether they were waiting down here for rescue, or a slow death.

Either way, it was going to be a long wait. They had supplies down here, the base was well stocked as an emergency bunker, so starvation wouldn't be an issue. However, the radiation from the bomb would severely hamper any efforts to rescue them.

Extricating herself from the wiring, Lindel walked over to where Jacinta and Jeff were waiting, each lost in their own thoughts.

"I think we're ready to try this," Lindel said as she approached. "If I've configured everything correctly, we should now have access to civilian satellite feeds. Outbound communication is going to take longer. A lot longer."

Jeff nodded. "Go ahead."

In the absence of a high-ranking military officer, by unspoken agreement the command centre staff were deferring to Director Illum's orders. Even though not formally part of the military, they all knew he'd been officially named co-head of their task force.

Lindel nodded back just as tersely. None of them were sure they wanted to know definitively what had occurred on the surface after the feeds had gone out. The only thing any of them wanted less was not to know at all.

Lindel moved to a nearby console and pressed a few buttons. The screen at the front of the room came alive with static and snow, and a low-pitched whine which set everyone's teeth on edge.

Slowly it brightened and, little by little, cleared. The first thing that became distinguishable was the bright blue banner of a news headline at the bottom of the screen.

Lindel continued to fiddle with the console's controls, and eventually the static cleared enough to read the text overlaid on that banner.

'Sydney City destroyed by nuclear blast!'

"That part we know," Jeff muttered.

"Do we have audio?" Jacinta asked.

Lindel looked up, but just shook her head.

She went back to manipulating the console, and the picture cleared enough to show a scene of utter desolation. Several people around the room gasped at what lay before them, a few even cried, but then there was silence.

Of the city centre there was nothing left, save a few charred foundations of some of the more sturdily constructed skyscrapers. Of the iconic Opera House there was no sign, and the harbour bridge was now a collapsed, twisted thing. Half-submerged on the far side of the harbour, the sections closer to the blast had melted away entirely.

To the south of the city nothing remained but a charred wasteland, all the way to the southern bank.

8:17

The loss of life must have been catastrophic, not to mention the economic and environmental damage that would plague the nation for years if not decades to come. And yet, the rampant destruction meant Project Emu had done its job well, or at least given them a chance. The question now was, had they deployed it in time?

The scene on the screen changed to a talking head and Lindel readjusted the console to tune into another station.

This time the feed showed aerial footage of the mass as it absorbed everything in its path. Then came the horrifying flash of the warhead and the blast wave which reached out further and further, overtaking the mass in every direction. The footage seemed to play in slow motion as Jacinta stood there with Jameson, Hially, and Jeff, mentally urging it on. In what must have been only an instant, the blast obliterated the original crash site. It surged outward and upwards in the all too familiar mushroom shape they had all seen on history shows as children.

At ground level the shockwave exploded outward in an instant, followed by the heat wall of the explosion itself, incinerating everything it touched. For long moments it stretched its grasp outward as though it had no intention of ever stopping, a force as inevitable as the mass itself. It reached the shores to the east, north and south, and eventually subsided after that into a red-hot smouldering wound that nothing in its vicinity could have survived.

"Did we get them all?" someone in the room asked out loud.

"Time will tell," Hially said circumspectly. "But I think, perhaps, you just might have."

A tremendous cheer went up in the room, more from relief than any sense of victory. The images on the screen showed all too clearly what this had cost, and it was nothing to be celebrated. They would live another day though, and for right now, for this instant, that was enough.

"I think we did it," Jacinta said to Jameson, whose arm had somehow made its way around her back.

The tall man still in his combat gear looked her right in the eye. "Yes Ma'am," he said with that slight smile of his.

She couldn't help but laugh, but then used her good arm to pull his head down far enough for a kiss.

He seemed surprised, but not at all displeased as he returned the kiss, and then some.

A small voice cleared its throat next to them and Jacinta disentangled herself in time to see Hially staring at them with a cheeky smirk.

8:17

"It's time I returned to my people. I can do no more here. In this thing you have either succeeded, or not. By the time my fleet arrives we shall know for sure. For what it is worth, I hope you survive."

The alien captain in the little girl's body lay down on the floor without further fanfare, and closed her eyes.

Jacinta frowned and looked at Jeff, whose expression mirrored her own.

A moment later the girl's eyes opened again, but now they appeared panicked, a panic which quickly grew into terror as she scuttled away from them.

"Ah," Jeff said in understanding before kneeling down next to where the girl had backed herself up against a desk.

"Sarah, is it?"

The young girl nodded as she looked around, ready to bolt at the slightest provocation.

"Where am I? Who are you? Where's my mum?"

EPILOGUE

Ten days had passed since Hially's consciousness had returned to her ship, and they were still stuck down here.

Two-way contact had been re-established with the surface three days ago. As yet though, no one had come up with a way to rescue the personnel trapped underground due to the lethal levels of radiation still contaminating the surface. There were talks of a lead-lined airlock and tunnel system to lead them away from the area, but those would take at least another month to enact. In the meantime, all they could do was wait. Tempers were beginning to fray.

Of the mass, there had been no further sign. It seemed Lindel's doomsday weapon had saved humanity after all, though at a terrible cost.

Jacinta had taken Sarah, the real Sarah this time, under her wing until they could return to the surface. The girl remembered nothing from her time walking the Earth with Hially's consciousness in control.

8:17

Despite everything she had been through, at least the girl was out of her coma. Apparently all the awakened had reverted to their former selves a few minutes after Hially had left. They were confused, and most understandably upset, but they were alive. The ones that hadn't been killed whilst trying to defend Earth at any rate.

It was strange. Jacinta knew she had only been involved in a handful of those deaths. Even so, she couldn't help but almost feel worse about those few than the million or more who had died in the blast.

At least at the end there had been a clear and imminent threat which required decisive action. All those of the awakened who had died in the A.T.U.'s, and other agencies' operations worldwide though could have been avoided. Their bodies' original occupants could have been restored to health as Sarah had been. If only they'd known.

She couldn't help but think of Victoria, or at least the alien pretending to be Victoria. She'd never known the real Victoria Jacinta realised abruptly. To all intents and purposes, the real Victoria's life had ended the day she'd been mugged and left for dead in an inner-city alley which no longer existed. And yet, without her and others like her which Hially's crew could connect with, they would all be dead now, humanity all but extinct. It was hard to feel bad about that, and made the entire aftermath even more confusing. They had survived, but at an unacceptable cost. Hially's people had targeted their most vulnerable citizens and exploited them without permission or remorse, even to the point of death, but in doing so had saved them all.

And in the middle of it all Jacinta and Lindel had killed more people than anyone else in the world for decades. How was she supposed to come to terms with that, even given the result?

"Director Illum, I'm receiving instructions from Canberra to turn on the news," a technician at a nearby console announced.

Jeff frowned for a moment before nodding for the tech to do so.

The screen at the front of the room crackled to life with the familiar blue news banner at the bottom.

No one was paying attention to the words overlaid on it this time though.

The word 'Live' was etched in bold letters at the top right of the feed. The rest of the screen was dedicated to a video of something massive breaking through the clouds above the decimated heart of Sydney.

The ship, and it had to be a ship, looked nothing like the crude constructions of human design.

8:17

Coloured a deep red, it was at least three kilometres in length, and maybe half that in width. Shaped like an elongated hexagon, it gave no consideration to aerodynamic properties, and yet slowed in a controlled manner, coming to hover several hundred metres above the blast site.

Everyone in the room gasped as a translucent blue beam shot out from the ship and began sweeping across the area, covering the decimated ground from one end to the other. When it was done, the vast ship angled to where the beam could begin on another strip of decimated land, where it repeated the process anew.

"What's it doing? are we under attack?" Jeff asked no one in particular. "Get me a line to Canberra. Now!"

The room buzzed with frantic activity as technicians raced back to their stations.

The feed zoomed in to a section of the ship near the bow and Jacinta stared at it for a long moment before smiling.

"Wait!" Jacinta called out to the now panicked room. "Wait, it's okay. It's Hially's ship."

The entire room just looked at her as she fumbled in her jacket pocket for a small piece of paper she'd been carrying with her for weeks.

"Based on?" Jeff demanded, still ready to launch into action if she couldn't explain.

"On this," Jacinta told him, handing over the slip of paper with four symbols written on one side.

"You remember when Hially gave me this in the interrogation room back when we still thought she was Sarah?"

"When she drew the star map?" Jeff asked, dredging up the memory.

Jacinta nodded. "Look at the symbols."

"Okay, but what do they mean?" Jeff asked, his patience at its limit.

Jacinta shook her head. "Specifically, no clue. But if I had to guess, it's the name of that ship."

She pointed at the screen, where the bow of the vessel was slowly turning towards them as it continued doing, whatever it was doing, to the ground above.

The morning sunlight shone off the alien hull as it hovered above the remnants of the city, and as it maintained its leisurely turn, four distinct symbols became apparent. Four symbols which matched the ones on the paper, stroke for stroke.

"I know what they're doing!" Lindel exclaimed.

8:17

"Out with it," Jeff ordered.

"The army went in and set up radiation monitoring stations a few days ago. I don't know how they're achieving it, but that ship is soaking up the radiation from the blast. I'm seeing a drop in levels all across the board. At this rate it will be less than an hour before it's safe for us to leave the bunker."

"They really came," Jameson said quietly from behind her. When had he arrived?

"I guess they did at that," Jacinta replied.

"Lindel, I want to know the moment it's safe to return to the surface," Jeff told her with a broad smile. "It's time to welcome Captain Hially to Earth. Properly this time."

Jeff didn't smile much, but when he did it was infectious, and Jacinta couldn't help but smile along with him. Today was going to be a very interesting day.

The End.

ALSO BY N. (P.) COOPER

THE PATH OF PRIDE

A PREQUEL TO THE DESTROYER'S WRATH

Scan the QR code above for more information!

THE DARK TEMPEST

BOOK 1 OF THE DESTROYER'S WRATH

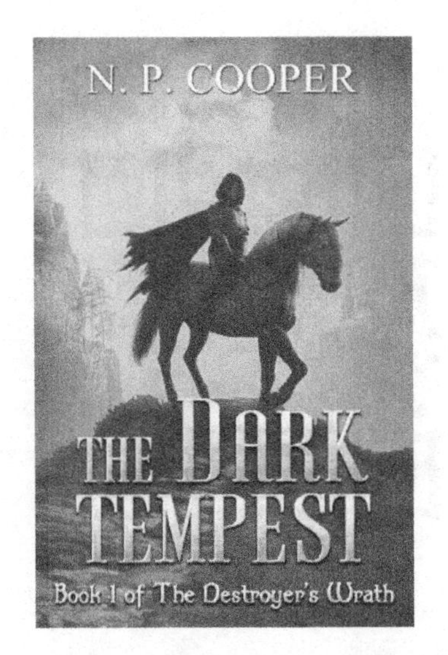

Scan the QR code above for more information!

THE INEVITABLE SPRING

BOOK 2 OF THE DESTROYER'S WRATH

Scan the QR code above for more information!

ACKNOWLEDGEMENTS

To my aussie writing group, thank you for your support. This book was a tough one to crack, and a lot of life happened while I was trying to get it finished, including covid, and child number four. I'm not sure this one would have ever happened without you cheering me on from the sidelines.

To my cover designer at 100 covers, your work on the cover was vital to the success of this book!

To the others who gave their time and/or effort towards the production of this book, your work is, as always, much appreciated.

Next up: The Day of Reckoning – Book 3 of The Destroyer's Wrath.

Until then. Happy reading.

Regards

N. Cooper.

ABOUT THE AUTHOR

N. P. Cooper grew up in Melbourne, Australia, and moved to Queensland early in his twenties. He has been writing for most of his life for his own pleasure, but 8:17 is his first novel in the Sci-Fi/Thriller genre. When not staring at his computer screen, he enjoys spending time with his family and friends, listening to live music, and exploring the local tidal pools with his children.

If you've read my other books you'll know I normally publish under N. P. Cooper. The reason this one is different is that I've decided to separate my genres with this distinction. My fantasy books will remain under N. P. Cooper, but my Sci-Fi and thriller works will go forward under N. Cooper to help easily define what genre my upcoming books will be in. As my back catalogue grows, this distinction will become more and more meaningful over time.

For more information on N. (P.) Cooper's upcoming books, appearances, and release dates, visit his website at www.npcooper.com

FOLLOW THE QR CODE TO
WWW.NPCOOPER.COM

Made in the USA
Monee, IL
22 February 2024

53940007R00184